# Finding Home

*A* **BAXTER FAMILY CHILDREN** *Story*

# Finding Home

# KAREN KINGSBURY
and TYLER RUSSELL

*A Paula Wiseman Book*

Simon & Schuster Books for Young Readers

NEW YORK • LONDON • TORONTO • SYDNEY • NEW DELHI

SIMON & SCHUSTER BOOKS FOR YOUNG READERS
An imprint of Simon & Schuster Children's Publishing Division
1230 Avenue of the Americas, New York, New York 10020
This book is a work of fiction. Any references to historical events, real people, or real places are used fictitiously. Other names, characters, places, and events are products of the authors' imagination, and any resemblance to actual events or places or persons, living or dead, is entirely coincidental.
Text © 2020 by Karen Kingsbury
Karen Kingsbury is represented by Alive Literary Agency, 7680 Goddard Street, Suite 200, Springs, CO 80920 www.aliveliterary.com
Illustrations © 2020 by Olivia Chin Mueller
Cover design by Laurent Linn © 2020 by Simon & Schuster, Inc.
All rights reserved, including the right of reproduction in whole or in part in any form.
SIMON & SCHUSTER BOOKS FOR YOUNG READERS and related marks are trademarks of Simon & Schuster, Inc.
For information about special discounts for bulk purchases, please contact Simon & Schuster Special Sales at 1-866-506-1949 or business@simonandschuster.com.
The Simon & Schuster Speakers Bureau can bring authors to your live event. For more information or to book an event, contact the Simon & Schuster Speakers Bureau at 1-866-248-3049 or visit our website at www.simonspeakers.com.
Also available in a Simon & Schuster Books for Young Readers hardcover edition
Interior design by Laurent Linn
The text for this book was set in ArrusBT Std.
The illustrations for this book were rendered digitally.
Manufactured in the United States of America
1120 MTN
First Simon & Schuster Books for Young Readers paperback edition January 2021
2 4 6 8 10 9 7 5 3 1
The Library of Congress has cataloged the hardcover edition as follows:
Library of Congress Cataloging-in-Publication Data
Names: Kingsbury, Karen, author. | Russell, Tyler, author.
Title: Finding home / Karen Kingsbury and Tyler Russell.
Description: First edition. | New York : Simon & Schuster Books for Young Readers, [2020] | Series: Baxter family children | "A Paula Wiseman Book." | Summary: For Ashley, moving to Bloomington, Indiana, is especially hard but with time, prayer, a few surprises, and especially the love of her family, she finally feels at home.
Identifiers: LCCN 2019007755| ISBN 9781534412187 (hardcover)
ISBN 9781534412194 (pbk) | ISBN 9781534412200 (eBook)
Subjects: | CYAC: Family life—Fiction. | Brothers and sisters—Fiction. | Moving, Household—Fiction. | Friendship—Fiction. | Home—Fiction. | Christian life—Fiction. | Bloomington (Ind.)—Fiction.
Classification: LCC PZ7.K6117 Fin 2020 | DDC [Fic]— dc23
LC record available at https://lccn.loc.gov/2019007755

*Dedicated to Donald, my Prince Charming.*
*I love you with all my heart. You are my best*
*friend, my home sweet home, my forever and always.*
*Also to my children, who were finding their way*
*when I began writing about the Baxters, and who*
*will now read these books to their children. And to*
*God Almighty, who continues to give me the most*
*beautiful life with all of them.*
*—Karen*

*Dedicated to the reader! This story is yours.*
*Never forget how much you have to offer this world.*
*And remember, there is always a seat at the Baxter*
*Family table for you! I hope that you find a bit of*
*home in these pages. Also, to my family—growing up*
*we moved quite a few times, and we always managed*
*to get through the transitions, because we had one*
*another. I love that I can find home with you all*
*wherever life takes us. And finally, to my Lord and*
*Savior, Jesus Christ: Thank you for giving purpose*
*and identity, and for letting me find a home in You.*
*May You be glorified in all I do. Happy reading!*
*—Tyler*

Dear Reader,

Wow!! We are so happy that you loved our first Baxter Family Children book—Best Family Ever! You made it a huge hit, and you were sure to tell us just how much that book meant to you. Thank you for that! The letters, posts, colored pictures, and reviews were heartwarming to me and to Tyler. One of our favorite comments was from a third-grade boy who said, "I will watch every day to make sure you write what happens next."

And so we bring you this second book in the Baxter Family Children series—Finding Home. Now that the Baxter Children have moved to Bloomington, Indiana, this book will give you a glimpse of how it can take a while for a house to become a home. Especially for the five Baxter kids.

Writing about the Baxter children and seeing them grow up in their loving and supportive family, has been an incredible joy for us. I've been writing about the Baxters for many, many years—the years when Tyler was growing up! Now, though, these books take us back to a simpler time when the Baxters were children, when they were growing up and finding their way. Sort of like flipping through the pages of a family photo album.

*Like with* Best Family Ever, *this second installment in the Baxter Family Children's story will have you laughing and smiling and thinking about what matters most—faith, family, and figuring out life along the way.*

*In fact we like writing about the Baxter children so much, there just might be a third book coming sometime soon!*

*Enjoy . . . and always keep reading!*

*Love, Karen
and Tyler*

**BROOKE BAXTER**—an eighth grader at Bloomington Middle School in Indiana. She is studious and smart and happy about her family's move. Like before, she has her own room.

**KARI BAXTER**—a sixth grader at Bloomington Elementary School. She is pretty, kind, and ready to make new friends—even if that means starting a new sport. Out in their huge backyard, Kari and Ashley find the perfect meeting spot for the family.

**ASHLEY BAXTER**—a fifth grader at Bloomington Elementary. When life gets crazy, Ashley is right in the middle of the mess. Always. She is a dreamer and an artist, open to trying new things. She sees art in everything, and is easily the funniest Baxter child.

**ERIN BAXTER**—a third grader at Bloomington Elementary. She is quiet and soft-spoken, and she loves spending time with their mom. She has her own room in the new house.

**LUKE BAXTER**—a second grader at Bloomington Elementary. He's good at sports, but sometimes he's a little too risky. Most of all he's happy and hyper. He loves God and his family—especially his sister Ashley.

# Finding Home

# 1

## *Far from Home*

### ASHLEY

Ashley Baxter tapped her foot on the car floor. Every interstate sign they passed meant just one thing. She and her family were getting farther away from Michigan. Farther away from her best friend, Lydia. Ashley slumped into her seat and stared out the window. All she wanted was to get out of this hot, stuffy car and run the other way. Back to Ann Arbor.

The only place she would ever call home.

She looked down. A blob of ketchup from lunch had landed smack in the middle of her white T-shirt, and the rest-stop bathroom paper towel had only made it worse. Her shorts were bunched up and the truth was, she'd had enough of this whole moving trip.

Ashley put her hands on her hot cheeks and leaned into the space between her parents in the front seat. "I'm feeling faint back here." She blew at her damp bangs. "Are you sure it can't get any colder in this place?"

"That's all we've got, sweetheart." Dad glanced over his shoulder.

A huff came from Ashley's lips as she sat back again. Fine.

Her parents said their new house in Bloomington, Indiana, was only six hours away. But it might as well have been a hundred and six. Ashley took out her sketchbook and studied her last picture. The one she had drawn as they left their old neighborhood.

A picture of their house. Their home.

Ashley breathed deep and rested her head against the window. She closed her eyes. Why did they have to move, anyway? She thought about asking, but she didn't want to ruin her family's happy mood. So she kept the thought to herself. A quick blink and she stared out the windshield. The trees along the side of the highway looked familiar. Her heart lit up. Maybe Dad had turned the car around at the last stop and he was secretly taking them back to Michigan. A smile tugged at her lips. It was possible, right?

A few seconds passed and the scenery looked different again. The truth hit hard. They weren't going back.

Not ever.

"Ten minutes!" Dad peeked back at Ashley and the other kids through the rearview mirror. His eyes twinkled and his smile was the happiest of anyone's all day. "Who's excited?"

"Woo-hoo! Me!" Brooke's shout came first. She was the oldest Baxter child and she sat against

3

the opposite window. Kari, a few years younger, sat between them. Brooke bounced a little. "I can hardly wait."

Ashley frowned. No surprise Brooke was happy about all this. She didn't have a best friend back home. No one like Lydia. From the rear seat, their two youngest siblings—Erin and Luke—clapped and cheered.

Ashley sighed. "I'm happy for you, Brooke." She turned so she could see Erin and Luke better. "And for both of you. My sweet young innocent siblings."

"It's gonna be great." Dad took hold of their mother's hand.

Ashley breathed a long breath. *Calm, Ashley. Be calm.* Maybe Dad was onto something. Wherever they were going, at least they had each other.

A big map stretched out across Mom's legs. A thick yellow marker line ran all the way down from Ann Arbor to Bloomington and it finished with a huge red circle labeled *Home!*

Ashley stared at that word. *Home.* What did that mean, really? If her family was leaving home, how could they also be *heading* home?

Mom's eyes got wide, and her voice was a happy squeal. "Take this exit, John. North Walnut Street . . . We're here!"

They left the highway and turned onto a city street. The trees were tall and thick with lush canopies of green leaves. Like something from one of their summer vacations.

"Okay, kids!" Dad looked in the rearview mirror again. "This is downtown Bloomington!"

"Look!" Mom pointed at one of the buildings. "There's a coffee shop and a farmers' market. And see down there . . . a little theater." Her voice trailed off.

The city reminded Ashley of commercials for Disneyland. Old brick buildings, bright-colored flowers, and neatly trimmed bushes. Families walked along both sides of the street, everyone smiling. Like something from a movie.

A butterfly feeling came into Ashley's stomach. Was she afraid or excited? She couldn't tell. The place looked special. A spot she might want to visit. The butterflies flew all the way up to her heart and a thrill ran through her.

Lydia would love this place.

They drove past a sign that read: SUNSET HILLS ADULT CARE HOME. The sign had an arrow pointing to a skinny street. Ashley tried to see what was down there, but their van was moving too fast. She liked the name. *Sunset Hills.*

After a while they turned down a country road that stretched into wide green fields and rolling hills. The houses here had open spaces around them. Very different from their neighborhood back home.

Kari began to bite her fingernails. She did that when she was nervous. "We . . ." Her voice sounded shaky. "We're going to live in the wilderness?"

"No, honey." Mom looked back and smiled. "This is the country. Our new house is in the country."

This detail made Erin and Luke and Brooke release another round of cheers. Luke patted Ashley and Kari on their shoulders. "I knew I was going to like it here!" He jumped in his seat a few times. "I'm Christopher Robin! With my own Hundred Acre Wood! All to myself!"

Erin giggled. "If you're Christopher Robin, I'm Piglet. Cause I'm little."

"I'll be Owl." Brooke raised her hand. "I'm the oldest."

Next to Ashley, Kari's smile turned sort of dreamy. "Then I'll be Winnie-the-Pooh! I can help you explore, Luke."

They all talked at once about how there would be ponds and toads and bunnies. Places to take walks and catch fish and look at the stars. A sigh built in Ashley's heart and escaped through her lips. "I guess that makes me Eeyore."

"Nah!" Dad did a half laugh from the front. "You'll be Tigger. One of a kind."

"And fun, fun, fun!" Kari grinned at her.

"Hmm." Ashley tossed that around in her brain. Before she could stop herself, she smiled. "Tigger is definitely better than Eeyore."

"Much better!" Kari put her arm around Ashley's shoulders. "Plus we can't be sad forever."

Dad turned the car left onto a long driveway and nodded at the house up ahead. "This is it! Our new home!"

"Wow!" Mom clapped. "It's beautiful."

The van slowed to a stop and Dad checked the road behind them for a few seconds. "Our moving truck should be here any minute."

Ashley studied the house. It was tall and white. Like a place where Pollyanna or Anne of Green Gables might live. A long porch stretched around it, and orange and yellow flowers decorated the front. On either side of the house there stood trees that looked perfect for drawing.

When they reached the house, Dad parked and everyone climbed out. Kari and Brooke ran up the steps onto the porch, while Erin and Luke took off for the backyard. Their parents smiled and headed for the front door.

Ashley crossed her arms and stayed planted near the car. She looked the house up and down and pursed her lips. "You're pretty." She squinted. "But you're not home."

Mom noticed her hanging back. "Ashley! Come on!" She held her hands up high. "What do you think?"

"I think"—Ashley whispered to herself—"it

looks like a castle." She walked up to her mom. "It's a bit big." She turned her head to one side. "I'm not seeing an actual house here. Maybe at a different angle . . ."

Mom stooped down so they were eye to eye. "I see what you mean. It's not the same as our other house."

"No. It's . . . different." Ashley bit her lip. "Which can be—"

"Good?" Mom finished Ashley's sentence and placed a loose piece of hair behind Ashley's ear.

"I don't think so." Ashley felt tears sting her eyes. "But maybe. Someday."

"Atta girl. Come on." Mom took Ashley's hand and led her into the house. "You're going to love it."

Inside, Kari raced up to them. She was out of breath. "Ash! Come see our room!" Then she took off up the stairs.

Ashley had no choice. She took hold of the wooden banister and trudged along behind her sister. One slow step at a time. At the top, she turned down the hallway. She walked past what looked like Erin's room on one side and Luke's on the other. Then Kari stepped out of the second door just ahead. "Wait till you see what I found! Come on!" She pulled Ashley into the room. It was a lot bigger than the one in Michigan and the ceiling was taller.

Also Ashley noticed a small purple stain on the carpet. At the other end of the room stood a window as tall as their whole room and beneath it a built-in bench.

"Isn't it perfect?" Kari ran to the window. "You could even sketch here! Come look."

"Hmm." Ashley took her time. When she reached the window she wrinkled her nose. "It's too big. No privacy."

"No it's not. It's beautiful. It looks like a princess window!" Kari pressed her nose against the glass. "Plus . . . we have so much space out there! Look at all we can see."

Ashley made a face. Five houses could fit in the front yard. "It's like a park." Ashley stared out the window. The only neighbors were very far away. The place really was the Hundred Acre Wood. "It feels like a hotel." She stepped back and crossed her arms. "Not a home."

"Don't be silly." Kari stared out again. "It's the best view in the world. Our own little kingdom." Kari had never sounded happier.

Ashley frowned. Who wanted to live in a lonely kingdom? And what sort of girl wanted a castle for a house? Her regular old bedroom was perfect and it was all she could think about. All she wanted.

Kari pulled Ashley to the closet and they stepped inside. "We could have a sleepover in here alone. It's huge!"

"True." Ashley kind of liked this idea. But not enough to smile. The best sleepovers were back home in Michigan.

"Look!" Kari put her hand on the closet wall and there, etched in pen, was a message. Kari read it out loud. "To the next person who lives here. This is the best room ever. Sorry about the carpet. My friend spilled purple nail polish. Love, Susie Macon."

"No wonder the place doesn't feel right." Ashley lifted her chin. "It belongs to some girl named Susie."

11

"Girls!" It was their dad calling from downstairs. "Come down!" He paused. "We have a problem."

*Great.* Ashley's shoulders sank. First she and Kari were being forced to live in someone else's room. And now there was another problem.

Downstairs Dad told them the news. "I'm glad we had the phone hooked up early. I just heard from the movers. Their truck broke down." He frowned. "They won't be here till tomorrow."

"Excuse me." Ashley raised her hand. "What if someone steals our stuff? I have important things in there."

"My best hairbrush is on that truck." Brooke crossed her arms.

Before Dad could answer, a thought came to Ashley. She cleared her throat. "You know, Dad . . . maybe this is a sign." She smiled politely. "We could tell the movers to turn around and we could meet them back home. Forget the whole thing."

The other kids started talking all at once until Dad let out a whistle. "Easy." He waved his hands a few times. "Everyone relax. We aren't going back. We'll order pizza and sleep on the living room floor."

"Pizza!" Luke cheered.

"And in the morning we can paint the back porch! That'll keep us busy till the movers come." Dad made it sound like this was a great change of plans.

Mom laughed. "Wasn't how I pictured tonight going, but it'll be a memory."

Then Dad walked to her and wrapped his arms around her. "Elizabeth, my love . . . we're home."

"Yes." Mom put her head on his shoulder. "Yes we are."

Watching them made Ashley feel a little better. But they were wrong about one thing. This definitely wasn't home.

The pizza arrived and after dinner they explored some more and then they made their beds on the floor out of sweaters and pillows from the car. Ashley closed her eyes and tried to sleep, but the noises kept her awake. First, a chatty owl and then a crying wind, which made the house creak. Suddenly a howl shook the air. Ashley sat straight up.

Wolves! Right outside the back door!

Everyone else was asleep. The moon through the windows cast strange shadows on the carpet. The house was empty and lonely and scary. Definitely scary. What if the wolf got inside?

"Dad." She whispered in his direction, but there was no response. She lay back down on her side and pulled her knees up close to her chin.

*Dear God. It's me, Ashley. I'm in this new house. And I think there's a wolf outside.* The moon was bright enough for Ashley to find her sketchbook. With quick pencil strokes she drew a different kind of wolf. Friendly and funny-looking. Then she waited.

The wolf was quiet now. *Okay, God. I know different isn't always bad. But please can I go back home? Someday soon? Thank You. Good night.*

Ashley didn't hear a response. But she felt better. God was always listening. Even still, the noises started again. Ashley opened her eyes and stared at the ceiling. She'd never be happy in this house. Not with the chatty owl. Not with the howling wolf.

And not when they were so very far from home.

# 2

## Painting the Porch

### ASHLEY

The morning sun shone through the window, and Ashley yawned. Mom's coffee smell filled the air, same as it used to every morning back home. Ashley sniffed and scrunched up her nose. The smell seemed strange in this big empty place.

She groaned and sat up. Not only was the carpeted floor hard and bumpy, but that crazy owl had hooted all night.

"Morning." Brooke sounded tired. She leaned up on her elbow. "How'd you sleep?"

"Not good." Ashley blinked a few times. "The wolves kept me awake."

Brooke sat straight up. "Wolves?"

Just then a loud beeping came from outside. Ashley gasped. "The truck!" She ran toward the front door and swung it wide open. The yellow moving van was backing down the long driveway with Dad guiding it closer to the house.

"Our things!" Kari joined them, and she and Brooke jumped around.

Ashley crossed her arms. She didn't want her things here. She wanted them back in Michigan. Where they belonged.

"It's finally real!" Brooke took in a deep breath. "Indiana air is the best!"

Ashley sniffed. The scent was grass and trees and hay. Like the Michigan State Fair. She wrinkled her nose. Home wasn't supposed to smell like a fair. Ashley turned to their mother. "Are we still painting the back porch?"

"We are!" Mom grinned. "Or I should say . . . you kids are." She moved to go back inside. "Oh . . . and your dad picked up breakfast sandwiches and paper plates. They're in the kitchen." She kissed Ashley and Brooke on the tops of their heads. "Come eat."

The other kids were awake and Dad joined them

for their first breakfast in the new house. They got to sit on the kitchen counter, which was usually not allowed. Already Luke was talking about the pond out back on their actual property. "It's perfect for tadpoles!"

Dad nodded. "The yard is bigger than I thought." He winked at Luke. "A lot to explore."

"Yeah!" Luke had the cutest grin. "I can't wait."

Brooke talked about how her room had the prettiest view for reading and Erin said she wanted to look for wildflowers out back. Kari pointed to the big window in the living room. "I can already imagine our Christmas tree right there."

Mom's voice was hopeful. "I prayed you kids would wake up seeing something good here."

Ashley drummed her fingers on her knee and looked around. *Something good . . . hmm.* Nothing came to mind.

Dad turned to her. "What about you, sweetie? So far, what's the best thing about being here?"

She thought for a minute. Slowly an idea hit her. "Maybe . . . painting." The idea made her feel a little better. "We get to paint the porch today."

She sat a little straighter. "Which is the best activity for an artist."

"I like it." Dad laughed. "I have five brushes and a few buckets of white paint waiting out back." He clapped his hands together one time. "Who's with Ashley? Hands in."

Ashley and her siblings giggled. They jumped down from the counter and formed a circle. They each put one hand in the middle, all together, like a sports team.

Dad and Mom added their hands. "One . . ." Dad smiled at the group. "Two . . . three . . ."

The whole family yelled, "Team!" Then they raised their hands in the air.

"Everyone out back." Dad grabbed the last sandwich. Then he turned to their mom. "Elizabeth, I think we're going to love it here." He tipped his baseball cap. "All right, Ash. Let's go!" He squatted low and Ashley hopped on his back. "Porch Paint Express . . . here we come!" He carried her to the front door. "I need a whistle! Come on!"

"Tooot Toooot!" Ashley pumped her fist twice in the air. She laughed out loud because something wonderful was finally happening in Bloomington.

They were having an adventure.

Sweat dripped down Ashley's face as she rested her paintbrush and looked behind her. They were getting it done. Almost two hours into painting and half the porch was bright white. She wiped her forehead with her sleeve.

Her siblings were slowing down, and Luke kept talking about the pond. Next to Ashley, Kari was painting about half as fast as before. "It's hot." She fanned herself a few times, and tugged at the collar of her shirt, like she would do anything for some fresh air. "I didn't think it would take so long."

Even with the heat, Ashley wasn't tired. She loved this job. Of course paint wouldn't make the place a home. But still, this was fun. She had never painted an actual building before. She dragged the brush slow and steady over the soft old wood. Every inch the brush touched turned bright white.

Like it was brand new.

Dad told them whoever lived here before had sanded off the old color and probably meant to paint it. But they never did. Maybe the family was too busy cleaning up Susie's spilled nail polish. Whatever the reason, they left a perfect opportunity for the Baxters.

A way to actually enjoy their first day in the new house.

Ashley focused. *Dip the brush, wipe it on the inside of the can, spread the paint on the smooth worn wood.* She had a system now. She bit her lip. *Dip. Wipe. Spread.*

Kari stopped and watched her. "You're good at this!"

"Thanks." Ashley felt her heart light up. "It's easy. Dip. Wipe. Spread."

"Hmm." Kari nodded and smiled. "I like that." She put her brush in the can and gave it a go. "Dip. Wipe. Spread. Nice!" She hesitated. "How do you feel today? About the move?"

"When the painting's done"—Ashley looked toward the driveway—"I might jump on the truck and head back home with the movers."

"You should stay." Kari sounded concerned. She kept painting.

Ashley painted another strip. "Maybe." She

stared at the fresh color. "Dip. Wipe. Spread." The words started to sound like a song. "Dip. Wipe. Spread."

Kari began to sing along while she painted. "Dip. Wipe. Spread."

Pretty soon Erin and Brooke picked up on the catchy tune. "I said a dip . . . a wipe . . . a spready-spread-spread!" Brooke put a little rhythm into it and that made her paint fly through the air like white raindrops.

Last to catch on was Luke, who actually stood up with his paintbrush and danced around. "Dip. Wipe. Spread!" He did a spin. And that spin spun him right into his can of paint and suddenly . . .

"No!" Dad came around the corner just as Luke's can spilled white liquid across most of the unpainted porch.

Luke stared at the mess. He lifted his eyes to their dad. "Sorry."

"It's okay. I'll be back." Dad was gone in a flash. From inside they heard him shout. "We need paper towels!"

Brooke and Kari and Erin stood frozen, their

hands over their mouths. Kari was the first to speak. "All that paint." She shook her head. "It's everywhere!"

Ashley watched the river of white move and spread over the unpainted porch. And suddenly she knew just what to do. "Hey!" She spread her arms out. "Maybe this is a good thing!"

Dad rounded the corner with two rolls of paper towels raised over his head. "Quick!" He handed one roll to Brooke. "Everyone grab some."

"But, Dad . . ." Ashley jumped in place, dodging the streams of white coming her way. "We can make beauty out of this."

He didn't hear her. The other kids grabbed strips of paper from the two rolls. Finally Ashley raised her voice. "Hey, family! Wait a minute!"

"Ash." Dad shot her a frustrated look. "Help us!"

If only she had a whistle. Ashley put her hands on her hips. "Someone . . . please listen!"

Maybe it was her tone, or maybe the way she was standing, but all at once everyone turned to her. This was her chance. "We're supposed to paint the porch, and now there's paint everywhere." She gave a slight grin. "Let's forget the paper towels." She shrugged. "How about we take our brushes and spread it."

Her dad blinked twice and then a slow smile moved up his face. "Brilliant." He laughed. Then he gathered up the sections of paper and put them on the nearby porch swing. "Why didn't I think of that?"

Luke let out a big breath. "So . . . I did a good thing?"

"I think so." Dad grinned. "Everyone grab your brush and start moving the paint around. Let's see what happens!"

Mom stepped out back and saw what was happening. "This looks like fun!" She grabbed a fresh brush from inside and lowered herself to the spot beside Ashley. Pretty soon the whole family was moving globs of paint down and around the wooden floor.

Mom laughed. "This might be the fastest anyone's ever finished a porch."

"Yes!" Luke raised his brush over his head. A dozen white drops hit his hair and his blue shirt. "I *did* do a good thing! I really did!"

Ashley worked as fast as she could. There was no dip, wipe, spread this time. They had to push the spilled paint over the porch before it dried.

And the plan worked! The porch was becoming snowy white before their eyes.

But that wasn't all that was becoming white.

Ashley looked up from her section and what she saw made her giggle. "Daddy's got paint on his nose!" She laughed a little more. "And, Mom and Luke, it's in your hair!"

Dad stopped painting and wiped at his nose. But that only made the white drop become a smear— all across his cheek.

At the same time, Brooke and Kari, Erin and Mom and Luke seemed to notice paint on their knees and arms and faces. Ashley, too. The porch was looking beautiful.

But the entire family was covered in paint.

Mom stood and held out her sticky white arms.

She had even more paint in her hair and on her forehead. "I'm covered!"

"I say let's finish." Dad grinned at the rest of them. "We can clean up later. This porch is almost done."

In hardly any time the porch was finished. Bright white and brand new. Twice as fast as Ashley's dip-wipe-spread method. She and her family stepped onto the grass and admired their work.

"Nice thinking, Ashley." He patted her shoulder. "Only Daddy's little artist could make something special out of a spill."

Happiness spread through Ashley's heart. *Daddy's little artist.* She liked that title.

Brooke ran and got the paper towels from the porch swing. "We need these more than the porch ever did."

Everyone laughed and wiped off whatever paint they could. Mom and Dad were still laughing as they headed toward the house with the dirty paint-soaked towels. "Good job, team." Mom looked back. "You kids take a break and explore. I'll make lunch."

Dad grabbed one of the half-empty cans of paint. "I'll finish the edges." He smiled at them. "You kids go on."

Brooke took charge and led the siblings away from the porch.

"Where are we going?" Ashley scratched the paint drying on her arms and cheek.

"Those trees." Brooke pointed to the far end of their property. "I want to see what's back there."

"Maybe there's treasure." Erin started skipping. "Or a portal to Wonderland!"

Luke jumped in the air. "Or maybe a bat cave!"

Ashley turned around and looked at the freshly painted porch, where her dad was working. She could still see the white streak of paint on his cheek, and a quiet laugh bubbled up from her heart.

Whatever fun things they did on that porch in the weeks and months and years to come, Ashley would always remember one thing. Her whole family covered in paint and turning a spill into something special. A mistake into a marvelous moment.

"Ash!" Kari called from the rest of the group. "Come on!"

"All right!" She turned and ran to catch up. As she did, she realized that something very special had happened. Something she hadn't expected.

Ashley Baxter had made her very first Bloomington memory.

# 3

## The Special Rock

### KARI

Kari waited for the others to catch up. She pointed back at the house, a thrill in her soul. "The porch is perfect."

"I know." Ashley ran to her. "I was just thinking." She linked arms with Kari. "We made a memory today."

Kari stopped and grinned. "We did! You're right!"

Up ahead, Brooke had taken the lead with Erin and Luke right behind her. Kari gave Ashley a gentle push. "See? I told you everything would work out."

"It's one memory." Ashley raised her eyebrows. "That doesn't mean I like the place."

"Oh, Ashley." Kari laughed. Her sister would come around. And this adventure would help.

As they reached the trees, Brooke stopped and looked back. "Whatever lies beyond this point is now our territory. Just us kids." She lowered her voice. "Whisper. In case any animals are hiding."

"Like wild lions?" Luke's mouth hung open.

"No, silly." Brooke laughed. "Like bunny rabbits and deer."

Kari watched Brooke pull back a tree branch and step through the small opening. A chill ran down Kari's arms. This was more like a jungle!

"Okay . . ." Ashley followed Brooke. She took a deep breath. "I'm going in." She climbed through the branches and disappeared into the trees.

Kari helped Luke, then Erin through the clearing. Finally it was her turn. She grabbed the branch, but the opening disappeared.

"Ashley? Brooke?" Kari peered through the branches. "A little help?"

Just then Ashley's head popped out. "Here." She held out her hand. "You have to see this!"

Kari closed her eyes as she made her way through

the rough branches, and kept them closed until she got to the other side. And there, in the middle of the trees, was the most wonderful clearing. She gasped. "Wow!"

A small stream ran down the middle of the open space, and rays of sunlight pierced through the branches overhead. Kari looked at Ashley and then at Brooke. "This is the most beautiful secret place ever."

Just then Kari spotted a bunny at the edge of the stream. Next to her, Luke was staring straight up at the biggest tree, and Ashley studied a leaf on the ground. Erin and Brooke dragged branches through the stream.

Each of them seemed mesmerized by what they'd found.

"Incredible . . ." Brooke broke the silence first. She spun slowly in little circles. "This really is Wonderland."

"Mmm." Kari leaned against a tree. "So peaceful."

Luke stared at something in the grass. At the same time, the grass rustled.

"A lizard!" Luke swooped the quick little green guy into his hands and held it out. "I present . . . Larry the Lizard.

Kari and her sisters screamed and jumped back.

A ripple of laughter came from Luke. "Ah, come on! This little thing won't hurt you."

They kept moving and stepped beyond the clearing through a second row of trees. There on the other side was an enormous rock. Bigger than their van.

"Look at this!" Ashley walked to the rock and ran her hand along the length of it. "It's not too tall. We can climb up."

She was right. Kari helped Erin, and Ashley helped Luke. In no time all five kids were sitting on the flat rock. Here there weren't as many trees. They could see the pretty stream and the forever blue sky.

"I love it," Brooke whispered. "It's a thinking spot."

Kari leaned back on her hands and stared at the clouds. "Thinking and dreaming." She could come here to talk to God about life and school and new friends.

Brooke sat criss-cross. "So . . . how is everyone?" Her tone was kind. "Honestly." She looked each of them straight in their eyes.

Kari pulled her knees to her chest. Brooke really cared. It was another reason why these were her best friends. No matter what happened in the new school year, they'd have one another. "I like Bloomington." She laughed and lifted her paint-splotched arms. "I'm having fun so far."

"It's just one day." Ashley leaned over her knees and looked around the circle. "Wait till winter. Bloomington gets so much snow people stay locked in their house for days, weeks even." Her eyes got wider and wider. "Wolves circle the houses! People run out of food, and they all get sick and forget how to laugh!" She paused. "A lot of folks can't take it."

Erin covered her face with her hands. "Wolves? I'm scared." She looked from Ashley to Brooke and then to Kari. She had a cry in her voice. "I don't want to run out of food."

"She's teasing!" Kari slid across the rock to the spot next to Erin. "Winters are worse in Michigan. It won't be like that." Kari shot a look at Ashley. "Right?"

Ashley looked like she got the hint. "Okay." A sigh came from her. "It's not that bad." She took a deep breath. "I don't like it here. It's a lot of change."

Luke smiled and held up his lizard. "I like it. I have Larry." He put the lizard close to his face. "I'm gonna get a bucket for him and feed him grass."

"Well." Brooke kept her serious tone. "I won't lie to you all. A new school will be hard." She stood and paced along the top of the rock. Then she stopped and looked at each of them again. "But we can do it. We're Baxters. We can get through anything." Brooke threw her right hand in the middle of them the way Dad had done earlier. "Who's with me?" She waited for a response.

Kari liked Brooke's enthusiasm. She stood. "I am." She put her hand in the middle next to her older sister's.

Luke joined next. "Me and Larry are in!" He

held Larry with one hand and threw his other one on top of Kari's.

"As long as the snow isn't too scary, I'm in." Erin stood and set her hand on Luke's.

Now they just needed Ashley. "Come on, Ash." Kari's hand remained near the bottom of the stack. "We need you." She watched Ashley process her decision. It was never easy for her.

Finally Ashley stood. "Let me make one thing clear. I don't agree." She made her way next to Kari. "All I want is to go home." She looked around. "But at least I have all of you. And Mom and Dad." She put her hand on top of Erin's. "Because of that, I'm in, too!"

This time Brooke led the cheer. "One . . . two . . . three . . ."

"Team!" They said it as they raised their hands high in the air.

Kari felt much better. They were in this together, no matter how bumpy life got. All of a sudden Kari saw a reflection of the rock in the water. Only this time it wasn't just any old rock.

It was theirs.

"I have an idea!" Kari almost yelled. "Wait here." She ran into the clearing, through to the other side and all the way to the house. Dad was inside now, and the porch looked completely finished. On the grass was an open bucket of paint.

She grabbed it and ran back to where her siblings were still waiting. Kari set the paint down and tried to catch her breath. "I brought paint!"

"Okay." Brooke angled her head. "For what?"

"The rock . . ." Kari couldn't contain her thrill. "This will be our new tree house."

Erin shook her head. "But it's not a tree house. It's a rock."

"Exactly." Kari dropped down and ran her hand along the smooth, cool surface. "A rock that belongs to us." She lifted her eyes to her siblings. "So it'll be *like* our tree house. Like the one we left behind." She gestured to the space around her. "This will be our new spot. Not just to think. But to hang out together."

"A new kind of tree house . . ." Ashley grinned. "I like it."

Kari put her hand in the paint and shook off

the drips. "This will make it ours." She bent down and pressed her hand to the rock. "Leave your handprint. Then use your finger to write your name."

Beneath her handprint, Kari scribbled K-A-R-I. Then she stood back and smiled. "Who's next?"

"Me!" Luke still had hold of the lizard. But with his other hand he made his handprint not far from Kari's, and he wrote his name.

Erin went next, and then Brooke. "I like this." Brooke's printing was neatest of all. "This will be our new secret place."

Soon, everyone—even Ashley—had a handprint on the rock. They stood back and admired their work.

Kari grinned. It looked perfect. The Baxter children had made their mark. But now their hands were even messier than before. She climbed down and washed her hands in the stream.

"Good idea!" Brooke joined her, and the others did the same.

The water was cool and deeper than it looked. Wonderful for a hot day like this. Kari grinned as she washed the paint off her hands and arms.

She pictured herself coming here all the time.

Suddenly cold water sprayed over Kari's back. She gasped and spotted Luke grinning at her.

"Think fast!" He splashed her again.

Kari shrieked. "*You* think fast!" She scooped water and threw it at her little brother.

Then Erin splashed Ashley, and Ashley splashed Brooke, and in no time all five of them were splashing and screaming and laughing. Before they knew it, they were soaked. Kari held up her arms. "At least the paint's gone!"

"Kids!" They heard the faraway sound of their mom's voice. "Time for lunch!" She shouted again. "We still have to unpack!"

On their way back to the house, Kari and Ashley and Brooke led the way. Kari shook the water from her hair. "I love our rock."

"Me, too." Brooke looked over her shoulder at Erin and Luke trailing behind them. Then she grinned. "Especially since school starts so soon."

*School.* Kari gulped. Moving here was one thing. Starting a new school was something else. She shoved the thought from her brain.

"Race you to the porch!" Ashley tagged Kari and took off. At first Kari tried to keep up, but Ashley was too fast. Besides, Kari didn't care much about winning. Not today. All that mattered was the adventure they'd just had.

As they reached the house, Kari looked at the sky once more. *Thanks, God, for that.* A warm feeling came over her because no matter what happened next, they were going to be okay. They would always be okay.

They had God and each other, and something else.

Their super special secret rock.

# 4

## *Kickball in the Rain*

### ASHLEY

Ashley had a theory.

If she didn't unpack her things, then maybe she could still change her family's mind and they could all move back to Ann Arbor before school started. She didn't talk about it with anyone else. Not even Kari, who shared a room with her.

They'd been in the new house three days and Ashley's siblings had already unpacked their clothes, books, and toys. And even though Mom was still working on things downstairs, everyone was amazed with how the new house was starting to feel more and more like home. But not for

Ashley. The place was like an acquaintance. Fine enough. Just not a friend. Not yet.

Probably not ever.

It was morning and Ashley could hear the other kids downstairs. She unzipped her backpack and found her favorite sketchbook. Then, like she'd done every morning since the moving truck got here, Ashley checked her best drawing. The one of their home in Michigan.

"I still miss you," she whispered. "Don't ever change."

Then she returned the book to its place and hurried off.

Down in the kitchen, Mom was balancing on a stepladder, moving dishes and containers from one cupboard to the next. "Why"—she sounded frustrated—"can't I get these shelves organized?"

"They look good." Ashley poured a bowl of cereal and sat at the table with Kari and Brooke. "Where's Luke and Erin?"

"At the pond." Brooke pointed to the back door. "They practically live out there."

Ashley agreed. The two youngest were obsessed with this place. Like they'd forgotten about Michigan completely.

Just then Dad bounded into the kitchen, the biggest smile on his face. "This is it! My first day at the hospital!" He poured a cup of coffee and looked at the girls. "How's everyone on this beautiful morning?"

"Perfect!" Kari gave him a thumbs-up and Brooke did the same.

*Terrible,* Ashley wanted to say. But that would spoil her daddy's happy mood, so she kept the word to herself. Instead she studied her father. "You sure look fancy, Daddy."

"Thank you." He bowed to Ashley and her sisters. Then he turned to Mom. "And what about you, my fair queen?"

"Me? Hardly fair." Mom wore sweatpants and a T-shirt. She laughed and brushed her hair back from her face. "I'm a mess."

Ashley studied her mother. Definitely a messy sort of queen. But it was nice of Dad to try.

Mom sighed and climbed down the ladder. She

42

faced Daddy. "You're going to love working here." She raised her hands in the air and then hugged Dad's neck.

"We need a send-off." Ashley banged her spoon on the counter. "Yay, Daddy! Dr. Baxter!"

Kari and Brooke cheered as well, as Erin and Luke walked in. In no time they were all clapping and cheering.

Dad threw his sunglasses on and did an Elvis-like pose, thumbs in the air and eyebrows raised. "Uh—thank you. Thank you very much!" He grabbed his bag and keys and pointed up. "And thank You, God, for my wonderful family."

Dad hugged everyone, but he held on to Mom the longest. He kissed the tip of her nose. "The kitchen is perfect. Just like you."

"Thanks." Mom looked more relaxed. "Have a wonderful first day!"

He kissed her lips this time. "Bye, my love."

"Hey!" Luke covered his face. "Yuck!"

"It's not yuck." Brooke smiled at their parents. "That's how marriage is supposed to be."

Ashley thought so, too. When Dad was gone,

Luke washed his hands in the kitchen sink.

"So, mister." Mom grinned at him. "Where have you and Erin been?"

Luke raised his eyebrows. His blond hair was sweaty and his cheeks had smudges on them. "We set Larry free." Luke propped his shoe on the closest chair and tied his loose laces. "He was tired of being inside."

Mom took a step back and studied Luke. "Who is Larry?"

"He's just . . . my friend." Luke made a nervous face at their mom. "My lizard friend."

Erin shrugged. "He was a nice lizard, Mommy. You should've met him."

Mom looked at Erin, then back at Luke. "You had a . . . ?" She leaned over her knees for a long moment. "We cannot have lizards inside." She sounded very serious. "Where was he living?"

"In here." Luke pointed to a dirty jar on the counter. It was very close to Mom's stack of clean dishes.

"Luke Baxter, that's one of my special canning jars." Mom moved it to the sink. "How could he breathe in this thing?"

Luke frowned. "That's why I set him free. He kept moving slower and looking more tired." He managed a slight smile. "It was time."

"Fine." Mom stood and stared at her cupboards again. Then she looked at Ashley and her siblings. "Everyone's unpacked, right?"

Ashley thought about slipping out of the room. Instead she focused on the milk at the bottom of her cereal bowl while her siblings all nodded their heads. Yes, they were unpacked. Mom told them they could wash their dishes and go play.

Only Ashley stayed quiet. Her heart pounded in her chest.

"Ashley?" Mom locked eyes with her.

Kari and Brooke each gave Ashley a sympathy look before they left the kitchen.

Ashley and her mom were alone now, so there was no way to hide the news. "I still have a few boxes." She lowered her chin. "In my closet."

Mom joined her at the kitchen table. Then she studied Ashley's face. "You were supposed to be finished by last night." Her tone sounded disappointed.

"I can't." Ashley blurted out the words. "I mean . . . I'm waiting." She shifted in her chair.

Mom scrunched up her face. "Waiting for what?"

Ashley rested her arms on the table. "In case we change our minds. So I don't have to unpack and then pack again."

This time patience seemed to come over her mother. She folded her hands and looked at Ashley. "We aren't changing our minds, sweetie. We're staying in Bloomington. This is home."

Ashley was about to explain at least ten reasons why this definitely was not home when the doorbell rang! The other kids came running in through the back door.

"Someone's here." Brooke pointed to the front entrance. "It looks like a family."

Mom made her way to the front door, with Ashley and her siblings right behind. Sure enough. There on the porch stood a smiling mom behind three smiley kids. The woman held a covered dish.

"Hi." Mom opened the door wide enough for Ashley and the others to gather around her.

"Hello! I'm Rachel Howard and these are my kids—Steven, Carly, and Marsha." She pointed to each of the kids as she introduced them.

"Well, hello!" Ashley's mom grinned. "Thanks for coming by."

Ashley studied the family. Steven looked old, like a high schooler. Carly was maybe around Brooke's age, and Marsha looked to be about the same age as Ashley. The kids' mother was still talking. And her stomach was big and round. Not like she'd had too much cake, but like she might have a baby in there.

"Anyway, welcome to the neighborhood." Mrs. Howard laughed and looked over her shoulder toward the road. "Not really a neighborhood. The houses are too far apart." Her eyes found Mom's again. "Either way, we live three doors down." Her words came fast and happy. "Just thought we'd stop by and introduce ourselves."

"That's so nice." Mom stepped back. "Please come in." She ushered the Howard family inside and shut the door behind them. Now it was Mom's turn to introduce the five of them, which she did.

"We don't want to impose." Mrs. Howard handed the dish to Mom. "This is lasagna. In case you're still getting your kitchen together."

Ashley couldn't believe it. How did Mrs. Howard know?

"Looks like I may get to return the favor." Mom gestured to the woman. "When are you due?"

"Two months." Mrs. Howard laughed. "But I'm ready for this baby to be here already."

Ashley did a quiet nod. Sure enough. Mrs. Howard was pregnant.

"You look fantastic." Mom smiled.

"Any advice for one more?" Mrs. Howard blew a wisp of hair out of her face.

"Be patient and don't rush!" Mom patted Mrs. Howard's arm. "And know you'll have help when the time comes!"

They made a plan to get together for a kickball game tomorrow and then the Howard family said goodbye. Ashley could hardly contain herself. She loved kickball. Still she watched them go with squinty eyes. They seemed nice. Maybe. Probably.

But the kids hadn't talked, so maybe Marsha had only come along because her mom made her come. Maybe she was a mean girl. She certainly wasn't Lydia. She probably didn't even know how to play kickball.

There was no real way to know.

Not until tomorrow.

Later that day, Dad came back to the house even happier than when he'd left. Over dinner he told them that he'd made a few friends, and met new patients. He couldn't seem to stop smiling. "I believe I'll be working there a very long time."

A sick feeling came over Ashley. *A very long time?* She pushed her fork around in her carrots. That meant one thing.

A move home to Ann Arbor was less likely all the time.

The next day the Howard family showed up right on time and everyone headed out front to play kickball. Marsha walked up beside Ashley. "I'm going into fifth grade." She gave Ashley a shy smile. "What about you?"

"Same." Ashley looked up at the sky. "Looks like it could rain."

Marsha shrugged. "Kickball in the rain is still kickball."

Ashley laughed. If Marsha liked rain *and* kickball, they just might be friends. Not like Lydia, of course. But it was a start.

They played four on four. Brooke and Carly played with Ashley and Marsha. And Steven played with Erin, Kari, and Luke. The moms sat in folding chairs and sipped iced tea.

The game was more fun than Ashley had hoped. She was next so she stepped up to home plate, which was an old pizza box from their first night here. Steven rolled the ball toward her and she kicked it long and fast. "Home run!" Ashley yelled as she ran to first, then on to second.

"Yeah! There's that boot!" Brooke cheered from the sideline. "Keep going, Ashley."

Ashley picked up her pace. She could hear Marsha cheering for her, too. A quick look and

Ashley saw Luke chasing down the ball. But it was a mile into the weeds. Ashley rounded third and ran for home.

Luke threw the ball to Steven just as Ashley jumped on the pizza box. "Safe." She spread her arms in front of her like an umpire. "That's a run!"

Steven jogged over and gave her a high five. "Nice job, Ashley!"

*Boom!*

Out of nowhere a huge crack of thunder echoed around them, and within seconds, giant drops of water came pouring down. The kids scrambled for the house, except for Steven, who grabbed the two folding chairs. Mom and Mrs. Howard followed the kids to the porch before the next bolt of lightning. But they were drenched. All of them!

Ashley wiped the water off her face. Marsha was doing the same and she smiled at Ashley. "Best kickball home run I've ever seen." She looked at Brooke. "You were right. She's got a good boot."

"Thanks." Ashley wanted to talk more, but the Howards packed up to leave. They all promised to get together again soon. Mrs. Howard even invited them to go out on their boat. "Lake Monroe is beautiful." She smiled. "You'll all love it."

After the neighbors left, the storm grew stronger. Mom sat by Ashley on the sofa and the other kids piled in around them just as more thunder shook the house.

"You know"—Mom spoke in a quiet voice— "after lightning, you can count until the thunder comes. That tells you how many miles away the bolt was."

A bright light lit up the front yard.

"I'll try it!" Kari counted slowly. "One . . . two . . . three . . . four . . . five . . . six . . ." *Boom!* She looked at their mom. "So that lightning was six miles away?"

"About that." Mom nodded. "But in a storm like this lightning could come at any time. Best to stay inside."

The rain came harder than before and Ashley settled in against her mother. Storms like this were the best. Like God was having a concert.

Ashley didn't want to like Bloomington or their house or anything about this move. But she had to admit something as she sketched herself kicking a home run that night in her room.

Today hadn't been too bad. She had made another memory. But more than that, she had made something else.

Her very first Bloomington friend.

# 5

## An Act of Kindness

### KARI

Back-to-school shopping was one of Kari's favorite times of year. New pencils and paper, a new notebook. Even sometimes a new outfit. But this year the time with her mom and siblings would be more than just fun. This shopping trip was critical.

Everything had to be perfect. The first day at her new school was just one week away.

It was midmorning and already they were in the van with their mom headed to the store. Sunshine sprayed bright light across the countryside near their new home. Kari looked out the window and smiled. So far she loved everything about

Bloomington. The house and the special rock at the back of their yard. The front and back porches and the neighbor girls—especially Marsha. She was in Ashley's grade, but she was closer to Kari's age. Marsha was kind and funny and she had a way of seeing the best in every situation.

So Kari and Ashley were already great friends with her.

Just yesterday Marsha came over and the three of them sat on the floor in Kari and Ashley's room. Marsha had told them about the Bloomington Fall Festival. "We make fall wreaths and paint pumpkins and take rides on a hay wagon." Her eyes had lit up. "Plus sometimes there's even a Ferris wheel and carnival games!"

Kari loved Marsha's enthusiasm. Their new friend was so excited about school starting in a week that Kari couldn't help but look forward to it, too. If only Ashley felt the same way.

They turned onto the main road and Kari looked across the van at Ashley. Later today she would check in with her sister and make sure she was okay. This change wasn't easy. But it was up to them to see the good in the move to Indiana. So much of life came down to attitude.

Like Mom and Dad kept saying, "Have an attitude of gratitude."

Kari looked out the window again. That's what she'd been trying to do. Find ways to be thankful. And it was working. The more thankful Kari was, the happier she felt.

Better to be happy with today than waste time wishing for yesterday.

Mom turned the van in to the Walmart parking lot and found a space near the front. "All right." She turned and looked at each of them. "I've got your supply lists from each of your teachers. Let's stay together. Okay?"

"Got it." Brooke was in the front seat next to Mom. "Are we getting clothes today?"

"Not today." Mom put her keys in her purse and opened her door. "We went through our clothes before the move. No one really *needs* anything new."

Brooke stepped out and shut her door, and Kari

and the others did the same. Brooke scowled as she walked beside their mother. "But . . . I *want* new clothes." Her words dripped with attitude.

"Your closet is *full* of clothes." Mom smiled. She definitely seemed to be trying to keep the mood happy.

"But it's a new school and—" Brooke hesitated as they reached the doors.

"Brooke." Mom clearly wasn't changing her mind. She swung her purse over her shoulder. "You have beautiful clothes."

"New is better." Brooke mumbled the words. She crossed her arms.

"Brooke." Mom was maybe losing her patience. "I need a better attitude, please."

Brooke sighed. "Okay." Her shoulders dropped a little. "I'm sorry. I'll have to make do, I guess."

Their mother smiled. "Yes. You'll make do just fine." She led the way into the store, and Kari stayed close to Ashley. "How are you?" Kari linked arms with her sister. They were still about the same height. But Mom said Ashley was going to be taller when she grew up.

"I'm giving myself some pencil time." Ashley lifted her chin. Her mouth seemed like it was trying not to cry.

Kari narrowed her eyes. "I think you mean pensive?" She giggled. "Like you're being quiet and thoughtful?"

Ashley stopped and turned to her. "No." She squinted her eyes and shook her head. "For me it's pencil time. That's how I say it. Pencil time makes the most sense since I'm an artist. It's when I feel like I could do a good pencil drawing because of my thoughts."

Kari shrugged. *Why not?* "Okay."

They were almost at the back-to-school section. Red and yellow and blue signs and banners marked the area. Kari felt a thrill run down her spine. School supplies were everywhere. "Well, Ash." She looked around. "If you need *pencil* time, you've come to the right place."

Ashley laughed. "That's funny." She smiled at her sister. "Everyone adjusts at their own pace, you know?"

"I know." Kari patted her sister's arm.

Mom pulled five lists from her purse. She handed one to Brooke, one to Kari, and one to Ashley. "Here you go. You older girls start finding what you need." She grinned at Erin and Luke. "I'll help you two."

Kari and Ashley stared at their lists, and Kari took a deep breath. "This makes it feel real."

"Yep. Unfortunately." Ashley sighed. "I hope I wake up." Her eyebrows lifted. "Here." Ashley stuck out her arm. "Pinch me!"

Kari shook her head. "No!"

Ashley slouched. "It was worth a try."

"Cheer up, Ash." Kari stood on her tiptoes. "Stand tall. A whole new year is ahead of us and I need my best friend by my side."

"Me?" Ashley whispered the word. Her eyes danced a little.

"Yes, you." Kari laughed. "Follow me."

Ashley let out a soft laugh. The lines on her forehead relaxed a bit. "All right. I'm with you."

"Good." Kari took Ashley's hand. "These are long lists!"

Pep entered Ashley's steps. "Adventure awaits!"

She skipped with Kari to the start of the school supply aisle. She held a pack of pencils up. "And this . . . is the perfect supply when you're feeling *pencil*."

They took packages of pencils and paper and pens to the cart and ran down the next aisle for binders and notebooks and folders. Kari picked one covered with flowers.

Everything from the list went into the cart, until finally they were running out of room. Luke picked a sports folder, and Erin grabbed one with a horse. Brooke's had stars and planets, and Ashley got one with the Eiffel Tower.

Kari smiled. She could have guessed that Ashley would get that one. Last year Ashley had called it the Awful Tower, until Dad told her the actual name. Either way, Ashley wanted to go there and paint one day.

When they were finished, Mom pushed the cart to the checkout stand. Kari could hardly wait to get home and sort through the bags.

Her siblings were talking about what they'd found and how they couldn't wait for school to start next week. Ashley's face looked happy, but she was quiet again.

That's when Kari noticed the woman in front of them in line.

She had bright red hair and a frazzled look. Four kids hovered around her and helped her unload her cart. School supplies and bread and milk. Kari watched as the last item made its way past the cashier and into a bag.

The cashier—a teenage girl smacking gum—looked at the woman. "Sixty-eight dollars and fifty-one cents, please."

"What?" The redheaded woman in front of them shrank a little and her eyes got as big as circles. "But . . . I gave you coupons . . . so it should have been—"

"I used the coupons." The cashier cut her off. "That's the price."

The woman peeled off three twenty-dollar bills. "That's . . . all I have." Her eyes got red and wet. She lowered her voice. "I . . . don't know what to do."

Kari held her breath. She saw that her mom was watching, too.

"Not sure what to tell you, ma'am." The rude cashier crossed her arms. "Either pay or step aside."

Kari bit her lip and waited.

"One second . . ." The woman rummaged through her cart, like she was trying to decide what to put back. She looked very nervous.

Kari's mom stepped forward. "Excuse me." Mom took out her wallet. "I'll pay the difference." She pulled out a twenty-dollar bill.

"No, no!" The woman turned to them and shook her head. "You don't have to do that."

Kari's siblings were still busy talking. Only Kari saw what was happening.

Mom smiled and handed the money to the cashier. "Please . . . give her the change." She smiled at the redheaded woman. "It could happen to anyone. Don't worry about it."

The cashier handed the stranger the change. For a long few seconds the woman only stared at the money. Then she lifted her eyes to Mom. "I don't know what to say." She brushed away a single tear. "Thank you."

Mom gave the woman a quick hug and talked to her in a quiet voice. "God sees you. He loves you." Mom smiled. "You're not alone."

The woman thanked Mom. Then she put the money in her purse and walked off with her children.

Kari couldn't believe it. Her mom was the nicest person in the whole world. They didn't even know the stranger. On the way back to the car, Kari looked at her mother. "That was really kind of you to pay for her."

"It was the right thing to do." Mom put her hand alongside Kari's face. "Like the Bible says: 'To whom much has been given, much will be expected.'" She smiled. "And we have been given very much."

Kari loved her mom for so many reasons, but this was now at the top of the list. The little act of kindness made Kari look forward to school. Maybe she could do something kind for one of her new classmates.

The possibility was something Kari thought about on the drive home and that night while

Dad grilled burgers. Their family really did have so much. Not just closets full of clothes and new school supplies.

But love and laughter and family nights like this.

# 6

## Ruined Hair and the Ice Cream Girl

### KARI

Kari had a secret.

Something about her hair that she couldn't tell anyone. Not yet. She locked the door of the bathroom she shared with Ashley, and stared at the mirror. How had this happened? The ice cream social was an hour away and Kari was running out of time.

Her hair was a disaster.

A loud knock came at the door. "Let me in!" Ashley's voice was whiny. "You've been in there an hour."

"Not an hour." *Half an hour, maybe,* Kari thought. Desperation filled the room like floodwaters. She

65

glanced around. A quick scramble through the drawers. Nothing. She looked along the counter for help. Still nothing.

The problem had come after she blow-dried her hair. Sure, it was clean. But it hung like a plain curtain around her face. A little curl, she had decided. That would do the trick. But Mom was the only one who had ever curled Kari's hair. And she had been busy in the yard this afternoon.

So Kari had figured she'd do the job herself. But not with the curling iron. That was off-limits without Mom's help. Then an idea had hit. Hair spray! After Mom used the curling iron she always used hair spray.

Maybe that was all she needed!

Moving quiet and sneaky-like, Kari had tiptoed into Mom's room and sprayed her hair better than it had ever been sprayed before. Then she hurried back to her bathroom and locked the door.

A quick flick of her brush and Kari had expected the curls to appear. That's what they did when Mom fixed her hair. The thing was, Kari wanted more curl today. Something older. Because sixth grade was the last year before middle school.

First impressions were important.

Instead her brush got trapped in her hair like a spider in a web. She tugged it and turned it and tried to get it out. But nothing worked. And now her hairbrush was so buried and stuck in her wild, matted hair she couldn't even see it.

Which was the secret she couldn't share even with Ashley.

"I just have to brush my teeth." Ashley knocked again. "Please, Kari."

*What to do?* Kari's heart pounded hard against her chest. Then at the last second she spotted her bath towel. She grabbed it from the rack, wrapped it around her head and flung open the door.

Kari breathed fast and hard. "Okay." Her eyes felt wide and nervous and panicked. "Your turn!"

Ashley stood there, arms crossed. "Why are you panting?" She wrinkled her face. "You sound like a dog."

"It's hot." Kari's heart raced like running feet. What could she say? They both knew she couldn't possibly have wet hair. She'd been out of the shower way too long for that. Kari tried to step around Ashley.

"Wait." Her sister blocked the door. "Take the towel off your head."

Before Kari could stop her, Ashley grabbed the towel and threw it to the floor. "What in the world?" Her gasp came quick and loud. "Kari! Your hair!"

"I'm ruined." Kari hung her head. "I borrowed Mom's hair spray." She lifted her eyes to Ashley. "I think I used too much."

"You look . . . awful." Ashley walked past her and grabbed her toothbrush. "You're supposed to ask." She squeezed toothpaste onto the brush and ran it under the water. The whole time she didn't take her eyes off Kari's hair. Ashley shook her head. "Mom's going to ground you for a year."

"That's why I had the door locked." Kari stepped back into the bathroom and collapsed against the wall. "How could this happen?"

Ashley started brushing her teeth. She turned and studied Kari, tilting her head one way, then the other. She spit the toothpaste into the sink. "You know . . ." Ashley touched the smooth side of Kari's head. "It's not bad. If you could find a way to even it out." Ashley smiled. She was clearly trying her best. "This look is in style I believe."

Then the worst possible thing happened. Mom walked in. "Hey, girls! It isn't long till—" Her gasp was even louder than Ashley's. "Kari! What have you done?"

"Time to go." Ashley flashed another quick smile. Then she darted out of the bathroom, her toothbrush still in her mouth.

Kari's words spewed like water from a faucet. "You were in the garden, and I couldn't use the curling iron. But, I wanted extra curls. Because sixth graders dress up for nights like this. Which is why I borrowed your hair spray, and now my hair is a giant fuzz ball and I look like a human dandelion." Kari grabbed a breath. That might've been her record pace for fast talking.

Mom touched the frizziest parts. "We can . . . fix it. Somehow."

Kari's heart sank. "No one will want to be my friend tonight." She collapsed in her mom's arms. "Are you mad?"

"No." Mom patted Kari's giant hair. "Come

here." She turned on the water and got her hands wet. Then she ran her fingers thorough Kari's hair.

"It looks like a tumbleweed." Kari felt like crying.

For a second, her mom looked into Kari's eyes. "It's always better to ask first." She smiled. "But in this case I think you already agree with that."

Mom left and returned with her hair straightener. "We need the big gun." She plugged it in and they waited for it to warm up. "Other than your hair . . . are you excited for tonight?" Mom leaned against the doorframe.

"Yes." Kari thought about it. "And kind of scared. I don't know what to expect. And I'm afraid I'll say something wrong or make some other mistake. Like the hair." Kari frowned.

"Kari Baxter." Mom put her hand on Kari's shoulder. "You are an amazing, fun, beautiful girl. You are going to have too many friends to count." She smiled. "Just be yourself." Her mom picked up the hair straightener.

"Okay." Kari could do that. Be herself.

After a few minutes, one section of Kari's hair was straight. The brush was still stuck somewhere in the mess, but Kari wasn't worried anymore. Mom kept talking. "Everyone makes mistakes." She took some of Kari's hair and set it in the straightener. "The key is to straighten things out." She grinned. "As soon as you can."

"*Straighten* them out?" Kari laughed. "Like my hair."

"Exactly." Mom worked the tool through another section and she raised her hand. "I can see the brush! We're getting there."

"Yes!" Kari watched her mother move the hot metal tool over the puffed part of her hair. Mom was good at everything.

Especially advice.

After a long while Kari's hair actually looked good as new. "It's a miracle." She turned her head one way and then the other. "Me and Ashley thought it would look like that forever."

Mom even added some curl at the ends. And then she ran and got Kari's pink headband! The one she had been missing! "I found this." Her mom stepped back and studied her. "There. You look beautiful."

Kari hugged her mom. "Thank you!" She

turned and got one more look in the mirror as her mother left the bathroom. If this mistake could be straightened out, then Kari was pretty sure she could survive anything.

Even being brand new at the ice cream social.

The Clear Creek Elementary gymnasium buzzed with hundreds of kids and their families. Kari and her siblings got their ice cream and saw Dad at a nearby table. Brooke had stayed home to organize her school supplies. Her open house was tomorrow.

When they were all seated, Dad looked at Kari first, then Ashley and Luke and Erin. "Well, what do you think?"

Luke held up his spoon. "It's a great place. I made three friends." He gave a chocolate grin. "I like it." The youngest two had already been to their classrooms.

Kari took a breath. "It's nice here." She looked at Ashley. "What about you?"

Ashley frowned. "I haven't met my teacher. Plus he's a 'he.' Which I haven't had before."

Dad sat between Kari and Ashley. He patted Ashley's head. "'He' teachers are very capable."

"Hmm." Ashley's finger tapped the table. "Maybe."

They finished their ice cream and Mom checked a piece of paper. "Kari and Ashley, let's go meet your teachers." She stood, and Kari and Ashley followed.

Their dad stayed with Luke and Erin.

Room 112 was just down the hall. Kari's sixth-grade homeroom. A sign above the door read: WELCOME STUDENTS!

"Here we are!" Mom walked Kari and Ashley into the classroom. The walls had one brightly colored strip of paper that ran around the room. It had a pattern of pencils, apples, and composition books. A woman approached Kari and Ashley and their mom.

"Hello! I'm Ms. Nancini. You can call me Ms. Nan." She bent down. "Which of you is Kari?"

"I am." Kari shook Ms. Nan's hand. Her teacher wore a beautiful green dress covered in pink flowers. She had a pretty smile and her dark hair was pulled back into a white headband! "I like your hair." Kari stayed close to her mom. She still felt a little shy. "It looks like mine."

Ms. Nan raised her eyebrows. "Why, yes it does!"

Kari introduced her teacher to her mom and Ashley. And Ms. Nan talked about what they would do in class this year. The teacher's eyes lit up when she talked. "And before Christmas we will write our own books!"

Their own books! Kari wanted to jump around, but she stopped herself. This was sixth grade, after all. "I love writing!"

"Good!" Other kids were waiting for her, so Ms. Nan had to go. "I like you, Kari. You're special." She waved. "See you Monday!"

Ashley's class was next, just down the hallway. Kari was glad their rooms were close. This one was busy with lots of animal and number posters on the walls.

A man walked up. "Hello!" He extended his hand to their mom. "Welcome to Room 107. I'm Mr. Garrett." He looked at Ashley. "Let me guess. Ashley

Baxter. New girl." He shook her hand next. "And please tell me there's at least a little ice cream left in the cafeteria!"

Ashley and Kari both laughed. Mom, too.

*A good sense of humor,* Kari thought. *Perfect for Ashley.*

They talked awhile with Ashley's teacher, and then returned to the cafeteria. Dad and the other kids were waiting for them.

"I think I need more ice cream. Chocolate this time." Ashley started back toward the line. She looked at their dad. "Don't worry. Ice cream is good for stressful times like this."

When she returned with a scoop of chocolate, she looked at Kari. "Your teacher is better than mine."

"Yours is funny!" Kari leaned her arms on the table. "He has a nice laugh."

"Well." Ashley moved her spoon around in her ice cream. "I'm still jury-out on the whole boy teacher thing."

Just then Mr. Garrett walked into the cafeteria. Ashley slouched down. "Do you think he'll make us run laps?"

Kari giggled. "No, Ashley! He's not a PE teacher."

The closer Mr. Garrett came to their table, the more jumpy nerves seemed to come over Ashley. Finally she leapt from her chair. "I see Marsha. I'm going to go say hi." And without waiting another second, she left with her chocolate ice cream.

Just then, Ashley's teacher walked up and introduced himself to their dad. The teacher sat down and talked about how he was looking forward to having Ashley in class.

Kari watched as Ashley left Marsha and hurried back to their family's table. She was holding her ice cream, and there was a paper plate on the floor in front of her. Kari could already see the disaster about to unfold.

Before Kari could warn her, Ashley stepped on the paper plate and started sliding.

"Ashley!" Kari stood up. But it was too late.

Completely off balance, Ashley slid and tripped and her ice cream dish flew out of her hands. For a second, Kari watched the dish spin through the air until . . .

It landed splat on Mr. Garrett's head.

Kari dropped to her seat and stared, right along with everyone else in the cafeteria.

Like a statue, Ashley stood—not moving—right behind her teacher. Her face turned a shade of red Kari had never seen before. Kari shook her head. *Poor Ashley. How could this happen?*

For the longest time, Ashley's ice cream dish sat upside down on top of Mr. Garrett's hair like a small white hat. Then slowly it slid down his face onto his shoulder and his dressy blue shirt. That's when he grabbed it and wiped the chocolate ice cream from his cheek.

"Ashley, quick." Their dad pointed to the ice cream station.

Ashley didn't answer. Didn't move. Almost like she was frozen in time.

Instead, Kari jumped up and ran to the ice cream table for something to clean up the mess. The second disaster of the day. Even still Ashley wasn't moving.

Kari ran the stack of napkins to Mr. Garrett.

People were still watching as the teacher wiped his face and shirt, best he could. Then he laughed. "I guess I'll be leaving." He didn't sound angry or embarrassed. He stood and looked at his shirt. "Chocolate doesn't go with this color." He waved at Kari's family. "I'd better wash up."

As he walked by Ashley, he smiled at her. "See you Monday."

Ashley's mouth hung open. She moved to the table, slithered back to her chair, and buried her head in her hands. At the same time, Mom covered her mouth and closed her eyes. Her voice got very quiet. "Ashley." She called after the teacher. "So sorry, Mr. Garrett."

The teacher saluted as he headed for the door. His entire head was matted with ice cream. Kari tried to stop herself, but a small giggle came out. Ashley's teacher was a good sport.

After a minute of silence at their family table, Ashley lifted her head. "I can never come back here again. Clearly."

Other people around them seemed to get back to their own business. Kari took Ashley's hand. "It's okay. Mom said with mistakes you just have to find a way to straighten them out." She winced. "As soon as you can."

Luke did a quiet little laugh. "It was sort of funny."

Next to him, Erin joined in.

"Thank you." Ashley nodded to their youngest siblings. "Glad to be so entertaining." Then she turned to their mother. "I need a redo. There's no way to straighten this one out. Unless we move back to Ann Arbor."

"Just tell him you're sorry, honey." Mom's voice was gentle. "On the first day of school."

Ashley tossed her hands onto the table. "The first day?" She rested her forehead in her fingers. "I'm extra-destroyed."

Dad patted her back. "At least you made a big first impression." He smiled a little. "He won't forget you."

"My future at this school has been decided. Forevermore." Ashley covered her face again. "I'm the ice cream girl!"

Something about that sounded funny and this time everyone started laughing. First Ashley, then Mom and Dad, and then Kari and the other kids until the whole family was having the best time.

As they drove home, Kari relaxed into her seat.

Everything was going be okay. School was about to start and there was no telling all the happy times ahead. And one day soon, Ashley would forget about the ice cream social disaster. After all, everyone made mistakes.

And Mom and Dad would help straighten out even the worst of them.

# 7

## *The Worst First Day*

### ASHLEY

Ashley pulled the covers up over her head and lay perfectly still. She'd been awake for an hour, maybe longer. But she couldn't make herself get out of bed.

Today was the first day of school.

Already Kari was up and humming in the bathroom. A song about being happy, of all things. Because of course Kari was joyful. She had not spilled ice cream on her teacher's head.

Just then a light came on and Ashley heard her mother's voice. "Breakfast!" She paused. "Happy first day of school!"

The covers stayed over Ashley's face. She did not move a muscle, not even her toes. Maybe if she pretended she was asleep, her mother would let her miss today. Instead, Mom sat on the edge of her bed and lowered her covers. When daylight hit Ashley's face, her mom smiled. "Good morning! Big day!"

Before Ashley could respond, Kari bounced into the room. "I can't wait!" She was dressed in her favorite jeans and shirt. She buzzed into their closet. "Where are those white tennis shoes? I can't find them."

"Top shelf, honey." Mom turned to Ashley. "What about you?"

"Actually . . ." Ashley sat up. There was no getting around it. "I have an idea."

A smile lifted her mother's lips. "What's that?"

"World travel." Ashley slid her legs over the edge of the bed. She might really be onto something here. "I think I should go around the world in eighty days. Like the book."

Mom tilted her head to one side. "That *would* be an adventure." She moved Ashley's bangs off her forehead. "But it's not an option."

"Are you sure?" Ashley felt sick.

"Yes, Ashley." Her mom stood. "Come on."

Another thought hit. "How about we stay here? You and me." The nerves in Ashley's voice sounded louder than her words. "I could brush up on my art skills and . . . you know, maybe help around the house."

"Ashley." Her mother took hold of Ashley's hands. "You have to go." She smiled. "Even if I'd like you to stay here forever."

Ashley climbed out of bed and faced her. "Mother. I don't know if you remember last week's ice cream incident. But it officially ended any chance of a good school year." She straightened a little. Her mind felt very serious about this decision. "Perhaps I could get a job?"

"Come here." Mom stood and pulled Ashley into a hug. "Today is going to be great." Mom pulled a navy blue pair of pants and a white shirt from the dresser and set them on the bed. "These are perfect." She sighed. "Trust God, Ashley. He'll be with you every step of the way."

"Maybe He could make me invisible. So no one remembers me as the ice cream girl."

Mom laughed a little. "That happened late in the evening. Most of your classmates were probably already home." She kissed Ashley's forehead. "No one will remember it, Ashley. I promise." She paused. "Plus there are a lot of kids in Mr. Garrett's class who don't know what a treat they're in for." Her smile looked extra-kind. "There's no one like you, Ashley Baxter!"

Kari skipped out of the closet. Her white tennis shoes were laced up. "Ready!" She grinned at their mother, and then at Ashley. "Hurry! So we're not late."

Mom headed for the door. "See you downstairs, Ash." Mom sounded like she was trying to stay positive. "It'll be a great day. I promise."

Ashley took a deep breath. *Fine.* She had no choice. With slow steps she got dressed and laced up her own white Chuck Taylor shoes. A ponytail might be best today. So no one would recognize her from the ice cream social. Ashley pulled her hair back and stared at the mirror. Mom was right. There really was no one like her. "Okay, God. Take me to my new best friends." She stared at herself.

Then she did a wink. "You can do this, Ashley."

Downstairs, Ashley ate three bites of eggs and a single piece of toast. Hunger wasn't her thing today. Then she sat on the couch and waited for her siblings. The extra time gave her a chance to grab her sketchbook and draw a picture of herself. She studied it. Yes, that was a confident look. She would use that one. Beneath the drawing she wrote, *Ashley Baxter: One of a Kind.* Then she added a dozen friends on either side of herself.

Ashley Baxter: One of a Kind

Because that was the plan, if only God agreed.

Dad dropped Brooke off first at the middle school, and the rest of them at Clear Creek Elementary a few minutes later. They were early, which was the best news. Ashley hated being late. Already she was the new girl who'd dumped ice cream on Mr. Garrett's head. Being late would only give the kids one more reason to stare.

*No one remembers the ice cream social,* Ashley told herself. She and her siblings walked up the steps to the school. Mom was right. Of course she was. She had to be. *No one remembers. No one remembers.*

In the main building, Erin and Luke turned down one hallway and Kari and Ashley took the other. "You'll do great." Kari squeezed Ashley's hand as she stepped into her room. "The ice cream social was forever ago."

Ashley shrugged. "Thanks." She gave her sister a quick wave and walked a little farther to Room 107. The bell wouldn't ring for another few minutes. So she peeked inside with just her head at first. The room was full of kids, all of them chatting and wandering around. Marsha was not one of them. Apparently she was in the other fifth grade.

That was the bad news. The good news was no one in here looked familiar from the ice cream social.

*Just breathe,* she told herself. She stepped all the way inside, and that's when she saw Mr. Garrett. His hair looked clean. He had recovered nicely from the ice cream disaster.

He looked her way, and she waved and smiled. Then he walked to her. "Good morning, Ashley." He squinted. "Let me see your hands." He waited. There was a twinkle in his eyes.

Ashley held her palms up . . . What would her teacher want to see?

"Good." He chuckled. "Wanted to make sure you're not hiding any ice cream."

"Mr. Garrett, I would never . . ." Then it hit her. She giggled. "You're kidding, right?"

"Well . . ." He grinned. "You never know."

Ashley laughed again. "You're funny, Mr. Garrett. I like that about you." She looked around. She didn't want any of her classmates to know about the incident. "Don't worry." She lowered her voice to a whisper. "I'll keep ice cream *out* of the classroom."

"And off my head, most of all." He gave her a high five. "Find your seat."

"Yes, sir." Ashley walked up and down each row,

starting at the back. She finally found her name on a desk at the front of the room near the door.

The exact place she didn't want to sit. Too much pressure to sit at the front. She tapped her finger to her lips and looked around the room. Maybe someone would trade her. She made eye contact with the boy behind her.

"Hi." He nodded at her. "I'm Elliot. I like aliens." He made some clicking noises and moved his fingers around. His voice sounded like a robot. "Take me to your leader."

"Hmm." She studied him. "Hi." Her smile took a second. "I'm Ashley Baxter." She held out her hand, and shook Elliot's. "I have a favor for you."

"For me?" Elliot's face lit up.

"I mean, not *for* you." Ashley shook her head. "A favor for you to do for *me*."

"Oh." Elliot wrinkled his face. "What's the favor?"

Ashley put her hands on his desk and leaned forward. "How about we trade seats?"

Elliot grew very still. He gave the front row a nervous glance. "Mr. Garrett said they are assigned seats."

Ashley frowned. Assigned seats? She hadn't had an assigned seat since second grade. Ashley sighed. Fine. She had no choice. She walked to the front of the classroom, where her teacher seemed to be getting his things together.

"Mr. Garrett." Ashley did a quick cough to get his attention. "I would like to request a window seat, please."

Her teacher turned to her and furrowed his brow. "What?"

"A window seat." She gave him her most serious nod. "That's actually my preference."

Mr. Garrett took a step toward her. "Ashley"— he shook his head—"this is not an airplane." He pointed to her desk in the front row. "Please sit where I assigned you."

Inside Ashley's chest, her heart pounded like a crazy drum. She pressed her lips together. "But . . . I do much better by a window." Her voice raised a notch.

"I'm sorry." Mr. Garrett shook his head. "Class is about to start. Take your seat."

*So mean.* Ashley kept the thought to herself. She

couldn't be rude to the teacher on the first day. Or ever. She hung her head and walked back to her desk. By now most of the students were seated. Elliot was talking to another boy about aliens. And a girl was now at the desk next to Ashley's.

Toward the back of the room a tall boy with brown swoopy hair stood in the middle of a bunch of kids. Making friends was clearly not a problem for him. Ashley looked again at the girl in the seat beside hers.

At the front of the room, Mr. Garrett was about to talk. So Ashley dropped to her seat and turned real quick to the girl next to her. She had a long braid down her back and her eyes looked straight ahead. Like she was more ready to learn than to make friends.

"Hi!" Ashley leaned close. She glanced at the girl's desk and saw her name. *Natalie.* "I'm Ashley. I'm new. How was your summer?"

Natalie took a few seconds before she turned and looked at Ashley. No words. Just a look. Then she turned back to the front of the class and folded her hands.

Ashley's mouth hung open. *How rude.* She was about to tell Natalie so, but there was no time. Mr. Garrett turned to the students. "Welcome to fifth grade in Room 107!"

For the next hour their teacher went over class rules and the things they were going to learn this year. The whole time Ashley couldn't focus. Natalie never once smiled, never looked at her. So what was the girl's problem? Why didn't Natalie like her?

Ashley thought hard. Maybe she could tell a joke to break the ice? Or she could comment that Natalie's braid looked nice.

She was still figuring out the right approach when the bell rang for lunch. Ashley walked alone down the hallway to the cafeteria. Not a single person wanted to walk with her. Ashley held her head high. It didn't matter. Kari's lunch was at the same time. Her sister was on her way.

Ashley took the closest table to the door and waited.

Sitting there by herself, Ashley noticed something across the room. The tall boy from the back of Mr.

Garrett's class, the one with all the friends, was holding his lunch tray and coming toward her. He walked like a sports guy. Concern bubbled up inside her. He seemed to be coming straight for her.

And sure enough he stopped right near her chair. "Hey." The boy smiled. "I'm in your class."

"Hi." Ashley wasn't sure what to say.

The boy gave his hair a shake to the left so it would move off his forehead. "You're new, right?"

"Yes." Was he actually trying to be her friend? Ashley's heart pounded so loud she could hardly hear. "I'm Ashley Baxter."

"Hi, Ashley." He studied her for a few seconds. "Didn't you flip ice cream on Mr. Garrett's head?"

*What?* Ashley couldn't believe it. This popular boy knew her secret! If there had been a way to dig through the cafeteria floor and burrow all the way back to her house, Ashley would have found it. She felt her cheeks get hot. "How . . . how did you know?"

The boy shrugged. "I was at the social. I saw."

Ashley crossed her arms. What a mean thing to

notice! "Do you think that's nice? To bring that up on the first day?"

Something in the boy's eyes looked shocked. "Uh . . ." He took a step back. "I was just gonna say I was sorry it happened." He blinked. "Actually, I thought you handled it well." He started to walk away, but he looked back over his shoulder. "Shouldn't have brought it up."

"Wait." Ashley stood. "What's your name?" She should at least know that much. So she could avoid him.

He stopped and turned back to her. "I'm Landon." He grinned. "Landon Blake."

"Well, Landon." Ashley lifted her chin. "Apology accepted."

Landon did a slight nod. He was still smiling when he crossed the cafeteria to his table of friends. So many friends.

Ashley crossed her arms. Why would he talk about the ice cream disaster? She looked his way. He was laughing and talking with everyone at his table. The heat in Ashley's cheeks grew hotter. That boy was probably telling his friends about the terrible incident. Everyone in class would know by the end of the day. Which meant one thing.

Traveling around the world in eighty days was looking better all the time. She put her lunch away and pulled out her sketchbook. She wasn't hungry anymore. For the rest of the break, even when Kari came and sat with her, Ashley drew herself on an adventure. Far away from here. She held the sketchbook out and studied her work. Yes, that's what she should be doing right now. Much better than staying here in this lonely cafeteria.

Now . . . if only she could find a hot-air balloon.

# 8

## The High Seas of Lake Monroe

### ASHLEY

A shocking thing happened over the next few days.

The rude boy named Landon apparently did not tell anyone about the ice cream social disaster. Because no one else said another word about it.

Still, Ashley was glad when Friday was over. This was Labor Day weekend! And on Monday she and her family had the most exciting plans since they'd moved to Bloomington. Plans to go out on Lake Monroe with the Howard family.

Ashley was the first one to the car that morning and Kari was second. "I've never been sailing!" Ashley had a bag over one shoulder. Sunscreen, sunglasses, flippers, goggles and a beach towel. Everything she needed.

"Me, either." Kari slipped her sunglasses on her face.

"Just think . . . in a few hours we'll be sailing the high seas." Ashley put her arms out to the sides and pretended to sail through the air. "I feel like a pirate headed for an adventure."

Kari lowered her sunglasses and peered at her sister over the top. "First, Lake Monroe is not the high seas." She giggled. "And second, you are a girl. And girls cannot be pirates."

"Yes, they can!" Ashley turned to Kari. "Girls make the best pirates."

Just then Mom and Dad and the other kids walked up with their beach bags. Mom raised her eyebrows at Ashley. "Who's a pirate?"

"Ashley!" Brooke folded her arms. "Pirates rob and steal things."

"Hold on." A terrible feeling came over Ashley. "Not like that. Of course not." Her family didn't understand. Enthusiasm leaked out of her like air from a popped balloon. "I'm a pirate who takes adventures on the high seas."

Mom watched them. "First . . . Ashley's right. Girls *can* be pirates." She raised her eyebrows. "But like Brooke said, pirates are generally criminals. Not the sort of thing that fits for us Baxters."

Dad patted Ashley's head. "Explorer. You're an explorer." He smiled. "I think that's the word you're looking for."

"Yes, Daddy." *Pirate* sounded more dramatic. But Ashley definitely didn't want to steal anything. She linked arms with Kari. "The two of us are about to be explorers on the high seas!" She danced around the driveway and Kari did the same. Ashley couldn't contain her thrill. "I can't wait to go sailing!"

"We're a family of explorers!" Dad got behind the wheel and they set out for the high seas.

A winding road took them through thick trees, and after a dozen turns, finally the lake stretched out in front of them. Ashley slid to the edge of her seat and stared at it. The water was the most beautiful blue canvas.

She shifted her attention to the parking lot. The place was busy. A line of cars waited to put their boats in the water. Apparently everyone was an explorer today.

As they unpacked their car and walked toward the lake, Ashley had no words—which didn't happen very often. The bright sun skipped along the top of the water, where boats raced across leaving a trail of white waves.

"There they are!" Brooke spotted the Howard family. They were in a truck near the front of the lot, and their boat was attached behind them.

Ashley stared at the huge vessel. It was easily a mile long. There were seats in the front and back, and in the middle they even had seats under a canopy. Ashley could feel herself becoming more of an explorer with every breath. Marsha was the first to run up to them.

"Hi!" Her long blond ponytail swished behind her.

Ashley and Kari and Marsha all hugged. "Guess what?" Excitement flashed in Marsha's eyes. "We brought our inner tube. I can't wait!"

"Inner tube?" Ashley squinted. "Is that an instrument? Like an indoor tuba?"

"No, silly." Marsha tipped back her head and laughed. She took Ashley's hand and ran with her toward the back of the boat. "See?" She pointed to a big yellow square raft. "Daddy pulls that behind once we get out on the water! We get to ride on it!"

"We do?" Ashley felt a slight nervous ripple. "In the middle of the high seas?"

Marsha gave her a funny look. "The what?" She shook her head. "Ashley Baxter, you're funny."

Ashley shrugged. She couldn't expect everyone to understand the way Kari did.

Steven drove the truck pulling his family's boat and got in line at the ramp. There weren't as many people waiting as before, and soon Steven, Mr. Howard, and Ashley's dad pulled the boat up to the dock. It was time to board.

The Howards' boat sat fifteen people, so the two families had plenty of room. Ashley stepped in. The floor rocked one way and then the other. "Whoa!" She steadied herself. This was going to be some adventure!

When everyone had their life jackets on, and their beach bags somewhere in the boat, the group set out.

"I know a spot on the other side of the lake," Mr. Howard shouted over the sound of the engine. "It's not as crowded."

Then he began speeding the boat across the water. The sudden thrill of it all rushed like the wind across Ashley's face. She wanted to stand up and stretch her arms wide. But she had a pretty strong sense that might send her toppling into the water.

So she kept her seat.

Around her, the others stayed seated, too, cheering and yelling about how fast and fun this was. Steven was the only one who stood. He walked to the seat next to the two dads and put his hand over his eyes. "I'll watch for boats."

Ashley liked that. Since they were on the high seas, Steven seemed like a good lookout guy. Every successful explorer needed a lookout guy.

Mom and Mrs. Howard sat together near the front. And the rest of the kids sat together at the back. Ashley tilted her head to the sun, excitement growing inside her. She could do this adventure every day.

Another boat crossed in front of them, and Mr. Howard yelled, "Everyone hold on!"

Sure enough, as they hit the waves from the other boat, they bounced three quick times. A spray from the lake hit Ashley's bare arms and her breath caught in her throat.

Finally they reached the other shore and Mr. Howard was right. They were the only boat in the area. He turned off the engine and suddenly everything was quiet. The boat bobbed around on the water as Mr. Howard left the wheel and faced the kids.

"Hey!" Panic ran through Ashley. "Mr. Howard! You still have to drive!" She stood. Her knees knocked together. "Please don't abandon ship!"

"Ashley!" Her father stared at her from the middle of the boat. "Sit down." He wasn't laughing. "That's not polite. You need to apologize."

"I'm sorry." Ashley sat down. She felt her cheeks get hot again. How come her dad wasn't worried?

There was no one actually driving the boat. She swallowed hard. Her whole body shook. "I'm . . . really sorry, Mr. Howard." She looked at the empty seat where the steering wheel was. "Would you like me to drive?"

"It's okay." Mr. Howard chuckled. "The boat's engine is off, Ashley. It's kind of like being on an island."

*An island.* Ashley glanced around. The shore was a long ways off. And other boats were crisscrossing the lake in the distance. She peered over the edge at the water, and then she turned to Mr. Howard again. "So . . . this is safe out here? Bobbing around like this?"

Marsha laughed and patted Ashley's knee. "Very safe." She looked at the other Baxter kids. "We do this all the time. It's part of boating."

"I wasn't scared!" Luke stood and puffed out his chest. He gave Ashley a look she might usually get from her father. "Boats always do this."

*Hmm.* Ashley was ready to move on to the next topic. She clapped her hands. "Okay, so what's next?"

"Tubing!" The Howard kids all shouted the word

at the same time. Marsha laughed. "It's the best."

Ashley watched while the dads put the big yellow raft into the water. Then Brooke and Marsha and Carly climbed on top of it. A rope connected the tube to the boat, and after hardly any directions, Mr. Howard began to drive the boat again. This time he pulled the three girls, who were screaming and laughing, skimming the water on the yellow tube.

"Hey!" Ashley leaned in close to Kari. She had to talk loud over the sound of the boat and the wind. "When did Brooke get so brave?"

Kari grinned. "I want a turn." She took Ashley's hand. "Let's be next!"

Ashley wasn't so sure. But she was definitely an explorer. Which meant being brave at times like this. She gathered her courage. Mr. Howard stopped the engine again, and he and Steven helped the first girls back into the boat. At the same time, Kari and Luke and Ashley jumped out onto the tube.

Ashley's heart thudded hard against her life jacket. When the three of them were situated on the raft, Ashley raised her voice. "Excuse me!" she yelled up to Mr. Howard. "What if the rope falls off?"

Dad walked to the back of the boat and peered out at Ashley. "It won't."

A million thoughts raced through Ashley's mind. "What if the tube pops? And we sink to the bottom of the high seas?"

Kari shook her head and Luke did the same. "It's Lake Monroe." Kari patted her arm. "Not the high seas."

Mom walked to the back of the boat, too. "You won't sink. You have a life jacket."

There were handles for each of them to hold, so Ashley grabbed on to hers. "Fine," she muttered under her breath. "Explorers have to start somewhere."

At first Mr. Howard drove very slow-like, which was nice. Dad stayed near the back. He yelled out to them, "How's that?"

Ashley felt herself start to relax. "Great!" she shouted. Then before she could stop herself she called out. "Faster! Let's go faster!"

Kari and Luke said the same thing.

Mr. Howard sped up the boat and with every

little bump all three of them laughed and shouted. The thrill was the best Ashley ever had. What had she been afraid of?

But just then Mr. Howard crossed over another boat's tracks. Ashley raised her hand to ask that they go a little slower, but as she did the wind picked her up and sent her cartwheeling over the water.

All by herself.

When the cartwheel ended, Ashley dropped into the waves. At first she wasn't sure she could breathe. Because the water was cold and little splashes kept hitting her face. Plus she was completely stranded, alone on the high seas.

"H-h-help!" Ashley called out. Her teeth were shivering, and she felt very small out here. "G-g-girl overboard!"

Apparently Mr. Howard knew there was a problem, because he whipped the boat around and came back for her. Straight at her. Ashley raised her hand out of the water. "Don't h-h-hit me!" She held her breath and waited for impact.

But Mr. Howard didn't hit her. He stopped the engine and the boat floated up to Ashley.

Dad and Mom were both at the side ready to help Ashley back inside. She climbed up a little ladder until she was in their arms.

Next, Mr. Howard helped Kari and Luke off the raft and into the boat.

Mom wrapped a towel around Ashley as she sat down. Dad stooped to her level. "Honey, are you okay?"

Everyone gathered around her. Marsha looked very concerned, and so did the other kids.

For a long minute Ashley shivered, not sure what to say. She wasn't hurt. She hadn't sunk to the bottom of the lake. And already she was safe back in the boat. Finally she felt a smile come over her face. "Did you see that?" She grinned. Who else had done such a thing? "I did a cartwheel on the lake!"

"You certainly did." Mom laughed as she stood straight again. "You're okay, then?"

Ashley nodded. "Is that an Olympic sport? Lake cartwheeling?"

Dad laughed out loud this time. "No, Ashley. It is not." He patted her head. "But if anyone could make it one, you could."

When it was time to eat, they pulled the boat up to a dock on the side of the lake. There were picnic tables and a field of soft green grass. After their picnic, Marsha and Kari and Ashley moved to an open space in the grass.

"Speaking of cartwheels, let's do some." Marsha giggled. She took gymnastics classes, so she was always flipping and spinning.

Ashley crossed her arms. They'd been over this. "I can't do a grass cartwheel." She smiled. "I do my best cartwheels on the water."

Marsha and Kari laughed. Then Kari put her hands over her head. "I've been practicing." She ran a few steps and her body went spinning like a graceful Ferris wheel. A perfect cartwheel!

"Wow!" Marsha clapped. "That's good!" She turned to Ashley. "Come on, Ash. Give it a try."

The possibility hung like a kite in her heart. Why not? Yes, she could at least try. "Okay." She raised her hands. Ashley pictured herself wearing a gold glitter leotard and red tights. A star gymnast. "Here I go!"

She ran and threw her body toward the ground.

But instead of a graceful Ferris wheel, she felt more like a lumbering bear. Her body slumped to the grass and her legs did a side shuffle. As soon as she was on her feet again, she raised her grassy hands in the air. "Ta-da!" She didn't quite nail it. Nothing like her lake performance. But she had tried, and that had to count for something.

As the two families packed up for the day, Ashley and the other kids ran to a group of trees where fireflies filled the air. The bug lights captivated Ashley. She loved how even in the dark, they had a light with them.

She chased one in particular and finally grabbed it between her palms. The bug lit up a couple times in the dark of her hands.

"Hi, little guy." She peered through the cracks between her fingers. "Don't worry. I'll let you go!" She opened her hands and the bug flew off.

Fireflies made her think of the light inside her. The light that came when she was kind or happy. When she did the right thing, like telling the truth or helping around the house. Ashley took one last look at the lake. She inhaled a deep breath. Yep.

This was her new favorite spot. The place where she had first tried boating and tubing and gymnastics on the grass. She laughed as she ran to catch up with the others. The important thing was trying. Whether exploring, or doing a floppy flip on the grass, or pulling off something she had never even known she was good at. Something she drew in her sketchbook on the way back to their house.

A perfect cartwheel on the high seas of Lake Monroe.

# 9

# The Cheater

### KARI

"Ten minutes!" Ms. Nan clicked her stopwatch and sat at her desk. Kari's heart picked up speed. The first pop quiz of the school year was under way. They had to finish twenty multiple-choice questions on the first two chapters of their history book.

And Kari hadn't read a single page.

She stared at the questions, and suddenly the letters all jumbled together. Why hadn't she made time to study? She felt sick to her stomach. Never in all her life had she failed a test. Kari Baxter was an A student. But the questions in front of her might as well have been in Spanish.

None of them looked even a little familiar.

Then something caught Kari's attention. Samuel, the boy in front of her. He seemed to be looking at the paper of the kid beside him. Samuel leaned over, and stared at the other boy's work. Next, Kari watched Samuel write something on his own page. And after that Samuel did the same thing again. Copying the other boy's answers.

Samuel was cheating!

Kari couldn't believe it. Ms. Nan had already said that if she caught them getting answers from someone else, they'd fail. No second chances.

Focus, she told herself. Time was ticking. *Come on, Kari. You know your history facts.* She stared at the questions, but still nothing looked familiar. She should've done her reading homework last night. Instead she'd spent the evening writing in her journal and talking with Ashley.

Kari's mouth felt dry. She could feel the minutes melting away. She looked up at Samuel again and paused. If he could get a little help, then couldn't she maybe . . . just maybe peek at someone's answers? She would read the chapters tonight and it would all be fine. She'd know the answers eventually.

111

At this rate she couldn't possibly get an A. There wasn't enough time, even if she could guess the right answers. And anything less than an A wasn't Kari Baxter–like.

Kari glanced at the paper of the boy next to her. Connor was his name. The boy never missed a history answer. By angling her head just so, Kari could see every one of Connor's answers!

As fast as she could, Kari circled the letters Connor had chosen. A. D. C. A. B. Connor was almost finished, and in no time Kari copied every one of his answers. Kari held her breath as she circled the final letters.

Wait. She stared at her paper. She couldn't have every answer exactly like Connor's. Quick as she could she erased one of the circles and chose a different random answer. There. Now no one would know where Kari's answers had come from.

Her heart pounded so loud she could barely hear the buzzer when it went off.

Ms. Nan stood. "Pencils down, boys and girls." She smiled. "I'll be by to pick up your papers."

Kari set her pencil down and sighed. She would live to see another day as an A-student.

Plus, she hadn't really cheated. She was just getting advance help. Tonight she would read her history book and she'd have the answers, no problem. Then she'd never miss her history reading again.

A loud sigh came from Liza Waters, the girl next to Kari on the other side. "I had seven left. That's so many!" Liza had the most beautiful curly hair. She wore the prettiest clothes in sixth grade and everyone liked her.

Kari kept hoping Liza would be her friend, but the two had barely talked. Until now. Liza turned in her desk and faced Kari. "My lifelong wish is to be as good at history as I am at everything else."

"Yeah." Kari smiled at Liza. She was confident, for sure. "That was a tough one." Kari exhaled as if she'd been working hard. "Especially the last question."

"Wait." Liza blinked. "You mean . . . you finished?"

"Yes." Kari needed to change the subject. "I did. True. But it was still hard." Kari couldn't stand to let Liza know where she got her answers. A distraction. That's what she needed. She pointed to Samuel and dropped her voice low. So only Liza could hear. "Samuel cheated. He looked at that other boy's paper the whole time!"

"No!" Liza's jaw dropped. "That's not allowed! I'm going to tell Ms. Nan." Liza started to stand, but Kari reached out and stopped her.

"Don't!" If Samuel got in trouble, Ms. Nan might catch Kari, too. "I . . . it's not our job to tell." She hesitated. "Ms. Nan will catch him on her own. Next time."

For a second, it looked like Liza would tell the teacher anyway. Then she settled back in her seat. "Okay." She crossed her arms. "I hope so."

Ms. Nan returned to the front of the room. She had a piece of paper in her hands.

Was this the moment? Was Ms. Nan going to announce to the whole class that Samuel and Kari were cheaters? She closed her eyes for a long moment. Why had she done it? What was she thinking? The weight of her cheating weighed on her like a small mountain.

Kari waited, but instead of talking about the quiz, Ms. Nan held up a sheet of paper. "Today at lunch there will be two tables with information about after-school activities." She walked to the first row of desks. "I'm passing out a list of options. I hope each of you will sign up for something!"

Kari was thrilled at this news! Finally! Now she could find out about soccer. Something she'd wanted to do since they arrived in Bloomington. But when Kari received the list she checked the front and back and her excitement fizzled. Dance. Jump rope. Basketball. Bowling. Horseback riding. So many things to do but . . .

"Oh, no," she whispered to herself. Then she tapped her new friend Liza on the shoulder. "No soccer!" She checked the list again. "I don't understand. You can ride horses after school, but no soccer?"

"True." Liza studied her copy of the list. "Soccer's in the spring."

Shock waves hit Kari and she felt her eyes grow wide. She was crushed. Ashley would be, too. Soccer was their favorite sister thing to do. "Well . . . this is devastating."

Liza giggled. "Not really. You can play later." She pointed to an activity halfway down the front of the page. "You should swim with Mandy and me."

"Who?" Kari still didn't have many names down.

"Mandy Ling." Liza looked over her shoulder. "She has the bangs. See, in the back row."

Kari looked around and a girl with glasses and pretty black hair gave Liza a thumbs-up.

"You'd love it." Liza sounded like the spokesperson for swimming. "Mandy was on the team with me last year." She looked at Kari. "It's the best."

"Hmm." This was tough news. Kari couldn't picture anything more fun than soccer. Her old school had an indoor field. Bloomington didn't have that. Then it hit her. Maybe she didn't deserve to play soccer. She was a cheater now, after all.

Practically a criminal.

The bell rang for lunch.

"So, are you gonna swim with us?" Liza nudged Kari. The two of them walked together to the back of the line.

"Maybe. I need to ask my sister first. She's in

fifth grade." They stepped into the hall and headed for the cafeteria. "Soccer's our thing."

The girl with glasses and bangs from the back of the class met up with them. "Hi!" She smiled at Kari. "I'm Mandy. Liza's best friend."

"Hi." Kari remembered to smile. "I'm Kari." She kept her eyes straight ahead for a minute. So, Mandy was already Liza's best friend. That didn't leave much room for her. She held her books tight to her chest.

Suddenly words from her father came into Kari's mind. *Be the friend you want to find.* Kari straightened her shoulders. Dad was right. So what if Mandy and Liza were already best friends? Kari could be their *other* best friend.

Even if she was a cheater.

"So, Kari. Where are you from?" Mandy tilted her head to the side.

Kari smiled. "Michigan."

"That's nice." Mandy skipped a bit when she walked. Like it was her own personal style. "We've lived in Bloomington for a while. But my dad is from China and my mom is from Chicago."

She grinned. "And Liza is from Atlanta."

"Yep." Liza laughed. "We're from all over."

"Exactly." Mandy giggled and linked arms with her friend. It was the kind of happy giggle best friends do. Kari wanted to be in on the jokes. She wanted it so bad.

As if Liza could read Kari's mind, she turned to Mandy. "Kari's thinking about swimming with us!"

Mandy gasped. "Perfect." Bubbles of enthusiasm came from her. "You should, Kari. You'll love it!"

Kari nodded. "I might." The idea was sounding better all the time. Soccer would always be her favorite. But since that wasn't an option, swimming could work.

"And wait till you hear what happened!" Liza looked from Kari to Mandy. "Kari saw the boy in front of her *cheating*! Samuel! He got his answers from the kid beside him."

"No!" Mandy made a face. "I can't stand that boy." She gave Kari a sharp look. "You should tell Ms. Nan."

Again, a terrible choking feeling hit Kari. What had she done? Not only was she the most guilty one by cheating, but she'd told on Samuel. And now it was spreading! She didn't even know the kid. Kari swallowed hard. What did her mom always say? *Talking bad about someone else only makes you look bad in the end.* The Bible called it gossip and it always hurt people. So now she was a cheater and a gossip.

"Well?" Mandy turned to Kari. She was clearly waiting for an answer. "Are you going to tell the teacher?"

"Probably not." Kari took a quick breath and shook her head. "If . . . if he's cheating, Ms. Nan will catch him next time."

As they walked into the lunchroom, Kari spotted Ashley at her same table with Marsha Howard. Ashley waved and just like that Kari's thoughts flipped again. What if Ashley didn't want to swim? They always did their after-school activities together.

Kari bit her lip. *What to do . . . what to do?* She and her new friends stood in line for their food. Meat loaf and gravy and potatoes. As they left with their trays, Mandy turned to Liza. "I forgot to tell you. The swim coach wants us to eat in her room today so we can talk about our first practice."

"Sure." Liza raised her eyes at Kari. Then she tossed her curly hair over her shoulder. "Come with us!"

Kari glanced at Ashley. Since they couldn't do soccer together, maybe it would be more fun to do their own sports this year. But, then . . . she couldn't do that to her sister.

"Wait . . ." Kari looked at Ashley and then back to Liza and Mandy. "I should probably ask my sister. In case she and her friend want to come." She started toward Ashley's table, and her new friends followed.

Along the way Mandy raised one eyebrow. "There aren't a lot of spots on the team."

Kari felt that sick feeling again. Was she supposed to choose Ashley or the new girls? The three of them walked over to Ashley and Marsha. Kari stepped up. "Um . . . Ash?" Kari looked at her new friends. "This is Liza . . . and Mandy. We're going to eat lunch in the swim coach's classroom. The three of us are going to do swim team."

"Just you three?" Already Ashley had a betrayed

look on her face. It didn't last long. She raised her eyebrows. "Fine. Go."

Kari shrugged. "I mean, you and Marsha could come, too." Kari looked at Liza and Mandy, and then back to Ashley. "Or . . . maybe you two could try something different?"

"I do gymnastics." Marsha nodded. "I don't like swimming." She turned to Ashley. "You should sign up for gymnastics with me."

"Yes." Ashley slid closer to Marsha. "Thank you for wanting me on your team, Marsha." She glared at Kari. "You're right. We can just do different sports this year."

Marsha looked happy. "Really?" She patted Ashley on the shoulder. "Best news all day."

Time was wasting. Liza was the first to speak up. "Kari! Let's go!" Liza was a bit bossy.

"Come on." Mandy took Kari's hand and started skipping her toward the cafeteria door. "The coach is waiting."

There wasn't anything left to say. "Sorry." Kari looked at Ashley. "I didn't mean you *had* to try something else." The new friends were leaving.

Kari had to go. "Never mind. We'll talk later."

Ashley gave her a sad look. "See ya."

Kari gave her a slight wave and ran after Liza and Mandy.

At the meeting, swim team started to sound more fun. They would meet at the city's rec center and have access to the indoor pool . . . even on the weekends! Ashley would've loved such a chance. Maybe Kari could still talk Ashley into joining, too!

But just then Coach Miller explained that after today's sign ups, the team was officially closed to anyone else. Which meant, no Ashley. "We have all the swimmers we need for this year." She looked around. "Let your friends know."

So that was it. Kari was on the swim team with her new friends, Liza, the friendly but bossy one, and Mandy, the happy bubbly one.

The three girls walked back to class together after lunch and Kari's heart was divided in half. It was the happiest day so far because she finally had friends. Real friends. But also she was a cheater. A crook. Something she'd never dreamed of being.

And she had kind of betrayed Samuel. And her very own sister.

If that wasn't hard enough, the craziest thing happened at the end of the day.

Kari watched Samuel turn to the kid beside him. "I saw your pencil was broken during the test." He shrugged one shoulder. "I kept trying to get your attention to give you one of mine."

The boy laughed. "I didn't know the answers, anyway. But thanks."

Kari felt the walls closing in. What was this? She had been wrong about Samuel! He wasn't a cheater at all. He was only being nice. And now Liza and Mandy thought he was a bad guy! Not only that, but her new friends didn't like people who stole answers. And she was one of those people.

Kari-the-Cheater Baxter.

She thought about telling the girls the truth about Samuel, how he really didn't do anything wrong. But then she'd have to come clean about her own law-breaking. Maybe if she just never talked about cheating ever again, everything would be okay.

Kari and her new friends walked together after class. Mandy was talking about her family's summer trip to Chicago. But the whole time Kari could barely hear her over the truth screaming in her brain.

The truth about herself.

Things got worse on the way home, when Ashley barely talked to her.

"Why are you being so quiet?" Kari whispered as they climbed out of their van and walked up the front steps.

Ashley didn't even look at her. "I'm surprised you want to talk to me since . . . you know." She turned to Kari. "You have other friends now."

"That's not fair." Kari's voice rose a notch. "I tried to invite you to swimming."

"I took Marsha's offer." Ashley tilted her head back. "At least she *wants* me on her team."

Usually when they first got home, the kids would sit at the kitchen table and do homework. But that would never work for Kari. Not today. She bounded up the stairs with her backpack and flopped on her bed. How had so many things gone wrong today?

On a day that should've been one of her best?

After a few minutes she stood and pulled her journal from her dresser. She sat cross-legged on the floor by the window and stared at the blank page. Then, the way it usually did, her pen began to tell God everything on her mind.

> I didn't try to hurt Ashley's feelings today. But here I am and now I feel like I'm carrying rocks on my shoulders. Ashley's mad at me.

She thought for a minute.

> Plus . . . I cheated on a test and I gossiped about Samuel. All of which I don't think were my strongest moments.

Her pen paused.

> But what choice did I have? I couldn't get a bad grade because everyone expects—

She was about to explain herself in writing when her bedroom door opened and Mom stepped in. "Kari? You sure were in a hurry to get up here. Why?"

"Because." She shut her journal and set it on the floor, fast as she could. "I have a lot on my mind."

"I see that." Her mother came in and sat across from Kari on the corner of the bed. Her eyes looked soft. "Ashley is being very quiet. I asked her if she was okay and she said I should talk to you."

A long breath came from the bottom of Kari's heart. "I said some things I can't unsay." The start of tears stung her eyes. She couldn't tell her mother about the history test . . . or Samuel. Instead she told Mom how she'd made two friends in her class and how she hadn't been very welcoming to Ashley when it came to the swim team.

"I told her maybe she should try something different." Kari hung her head.

For a few seconds her mother didn't say anything. When she did her voice was patient. "Did you really want Ashley to sign up for swimming?"

"Not really." Kari needed to tell the truth here. "I thought it might be fun if I had my own sport with my *new* friends." A warm tear slid down her cheek. "I didn't know how to tell her, Mom. It was just . . . with my friends there, it felt kind of mean." She did a loud breath. "Just trying to figure out how to do this."

Her mom lowered herself to the spot beside Kari on the floor. She took hold of Kari's hand. "Maybe you were trying to impress those girls. What do you think?"

"Maybe." The memory of the other situation came to her brain. "Also . . . I saw this boy cheating on our pop quiz. Or that's what I thought, anyway." A tear slid down her other cheek. She could at least be honest about this part. "I had that interesting news, so I told both the girls—Liza and Mandy."

Suddenly she remembered what Mandy had said. *I can't stand that boy.* And Kari's tears came like rain. "I found out later that the boy was only trying to help some kid with a new pencil." A couple quiet sobs shook her chest. Because even now she couldn't tell her mother she was a cheater. "And now Liza and Mandy think he's a bad kid. And it's all my fault."

Kari covered her face with her hands. After a few seconds she felt her mother's arm come around her shoulders. It took a minute, but finally her tears slowed down. Kari lowered her hands and looked into her mom's eyes. "What should I do?"

"Well . . . you're right. You can't unsay those things, honey. But there is something you can do." Mom put her hand along Kari's cheek and used her thumb to wipe away some of Kari's tears. "You can apologize to Ashley. And you can tell Liza and Mandy the truth about Samuel."

Kari's heart still hurt even though she wasn't crying anymore. The rocks remained. "Yes." She gave her mom a sad look. "I can do those things."

Mom's smile started in her eyes. "That's my girl." She turned a little so they were facing each other. "Now you see why we don't talk bad about other people." She reached out and took hold of Kari's hands. "God wants us to use our words to spread kindness and love."

Why hadn't she thought of that before? Kari nodded. "What about Ashley?"

"Just talk to her. And remember something,

sweetie." Her mom paused. "You barely know those girls. Ashley is your best friend. She always will be."

Her mother was completely right. If only Kari could tell the truth about her own cheating. But that would make her a criminal, and she didn't ever want her family to think of her that way. She took a slow breath. "Thank you. I needed to hear that. About Ashley." Kari didn't want to look into her mother's eyes very long. Not with all the rocks. Also she wasn't sure she had the strength to go back downstairs. She might start crying again. "Can you ask Ashley to come up here? I need to talk to her."

"Sure." Her mom leaned close and kissed Kari's cheek. "It'll all be fine. Remember, an apology builds a bridge between two people who have distance."

"I love you, Mom." Kari stood and a quiet voice whispered in her heart. *Tell her the truth. Tell your mother about the cheating.* But Kari refused to listen.

Even so, her mother hugged her. After a few seconds Kari looked up. "How did you know I needed you just now?"

This time her mom's smile looked happy. Like

everything really would be okay. "That's a mother's job. To know when her kids need her."

Kari watched her mom go. Her heart should feel lighter, but it didn't. It was the first time she hadn't told her mother the whole truth. And she had the most wonderful mother.

Yes, in a few minutes she would apologize to Ashley and they would be best friends again. Then tomorrow she would tell Liza and Mandy the truth about Samuel. After that she would be more careful about her words. Because once they're said, there's no way to unsay them. Not ever.

But none of that would change the one fact she wasn't willing to talk about.

Kari Baxter was a cheater.

# 10

## The Mud, the Menace, and the Mentos

### ASHLEY

Ashley wasn't sure if she was awake or not. She was in her bed, and she could hear the storm outside. But instead of Bloomington, she was back home in Ann Arbor. Her old walls surrounded her, and she could smell the familiar air. The rain sounded just like it had in Michigan. She felt warm and wonderful and cozy.

But then bit by bit Ashley opened her eyes and looked around. Her heart sank to her feet. No, she was not home, after all. She was here.

In the big, cold bedroom in Bloomington.

Ashley sat up. Water pelted the window like popcorn.

Normally, today would mean wearing rain boots

131

to school. But Mom had announced last night that their boots were still in the unpacked boxes in the garage. So, the Baxter children were stuck wearing tennis shoes.

The problem came when Mom dropped them off.

One minute Ashley was waving goodbye to her mother, not paying attention to the ground, and the next, she stepped right in the middle of a deep muddy puddle. She gasped and looked down. "No! This can't be happening." Both her pretty white shoes were covered in mud.

Luke and Erin ran to their classes. Only Kari stayed to see how the muddy shoes tragedy was going to play out. She stared at Ashley's shoes. "That's a lot of mud."

"I'm a disaster, Kari. A muddy mess." Ashley put her feet out in front of her and leaned back.

"Ash, you're getting soaked." Kari covered her smile with her hand. "What are you doing?"

"Cleaning myself." Ashley leaned back a little more and then something even worse happened. She started to fall. At the last second she threw herself forward and her knees landed in the same mud puddle. Ashley looked up from her spot on the ground. "I might need to call in sick today. Mud fever."

Kari helped Ashley to her feet just as the first bell rang.

"We have to go!" Kari sounded panicked. She hated being late as much as Ashley did. She helped Ashley into the restroom and the two of them used paper towels to clean up the clumps. Mud streaks were everywhere. Ashley's shoes and knees and her raincoat and pink shirt.

The girls did their best, but it wasn't enough.

Kari stepped back and studied her. "At least you're dry. And your face and hands are clean."

"The ground never got this muddy when it rained back home." Ashley frowned. If they had just stayed in Ann Arbor, then she wouldn't be in this mess. Literally.

They tossed the dirty paper towels in the trash and hurried down their hallway. Kari gave her a last look. "It'll be okay." She patted Ashley's shoulder and then darted into her classroom.

Ashley put her backpack in front of her so she could hide the smudges. Then she walked into the room, slinked to her desk, and sat down without anyone seeming to notice her muddy condition. Which felt like a miracle.

A minute later Natalie took her seat. Natalie, the rude girl with the braid who sat right beside her but never said a word. Ashley studied Natalie. As rude as the girl was, Ashley still wanted to be her friend. Because Natalie wasn't only rude to Ashley. The girl didn't talk to anyone. She seemed to need a friend as much as Ashley did.

But becoming that friend was not turning out to be an easy job.

That's when Ashley remembered what her mom had said last night about the situation. *Give a compliment or ask a question. Say something kind.* Mom's suggestion seemed impossible, especially with the way Natalie was acting.

The girl wore yellow rain boots and a white-flowered headband. Maybe a compliment about Natalie's outfit would help. Ashley was about to do just that when she paused. Perhaps she should pick a nonmuddy day to make her next attempt at friendship.

Mr. Garrett took the front of the class. "Like I told you," he said, "today you will be assigned your sea animal for our science reports."

*Sea animals?* Suddenly, Ashley's muddy mood lifted. There was a chance this day could get better. All week Ashley had hinted to her teacher that she would like a dolphin or a sea turtle. She held her breath as Mr. Garrett handed each student a piece of paper with their animal. Ashley could almost see the words before her teacher reached her.

*Dolphin. Sea Turtle. Please!*

Instead the teacher handed Ashley a page with the image of a slimy, unattractive octopus. Ashley furrowed her brow and shot a look at her teacher. "Umm. Sir. Did you get my hints? About the dolphin or turtle?"

"Yes." He smiled at her. "But I gave you the octopus, Ashley." He hesitated. "I think you'll enjoy researching an animal you're less familiar with."

Ashley stared at the image. "So many . . . legs."

"Yes." Mr. Garrett laughed. "And you get to learn about how the octopus uses those legs." He patted her shoulder and moved on.

Ashley studied the octopus on her handout. Maybe this creature wasn't so bad. His head was big, so probably he was the smartest of the sea animals. That could possibly be interesting.

When the lunch bell rang, Ashley felt proud of herself. Three awful events today. The mud, the silent treatment from Natalie, and the octopus. And she hadn't even cried.

Not a single tear.

*Face high,* she told herself. She was Ashley Baxter and she could wear mud better than anyone. She could sit next to the mean girl and still have a good day, and she could miss out on the dolphin and sea turtle and find a way to like an octopus.

*Look for the good,* she thought. Something her dad was always telling them to do.

But just then someone behind her in the hallway called her name. The voice belonged to a boy. Ashley didn't have to turn around to know who it was.

Landon Blake.

"Psssst. Ashley." He came closer. "I'm talking to you."

She spun around and looked straight at him. "What do *you* want?" Ashley whispered back. She didn't want to get in trouble for being loud in the hall.

He smiled a goofy sort of secret smile. "Your shoe's untied." Landon pointed down at her feet. "Look!"

How could this be happening? Her shoes were muddy *and* untied? Really? She looked down. But they weren't actually untied at all. They were still perfectly laced.

"Made you look!" Landon laughed. His eyes were sort of sparkly. "Funny, right?"

"No." Ashley gave him the same look she'd given the octopus a few minutes ago. "I have a suggestion, Landon Blake."

"Okay." He started walking beside her. "I have to hear this."

She stopped again and studied him. "Don't be a comedian."

This time he laughed harder. Like they were

friends or something. "You're spunky."

Was that supposed to be a compliment? Ashley resumed walking and Landon kept up. "I got a sea turtle for the project." He glanced at her. "What did you get?"

"An octopus." Ashley could hardly wait to find Marsha at their table. This conversation was getting on her nerves. It was not fair that Landon got a sea turtle. She used her most professional tone. "And the octopus is the best because . . . eight legs, naturally. Nothing else has that."

"Except spiders." Landon grinned at her.

That was it. Landon Blake was officially a menace.

Ashley stopped and put her hands on her hips. "I really hope you don't embarrass yourself when you present your sea turtle project." She tilted her head. "You don't seem like a very mature fifth grader."

"Oh . . . like you? Who fell in the mud today?" Landon pointed at her. "That's pretty immature, if you ask me."

"No one asked you." She had no choice but to stay confident here.

"Whatever you say, Ashley." Landon laughed and kept walking. He looked back just once. "Keep being spunky. It suits you."

She stared at him as he walked to the boys' table on the other side of the cafeteria. But she had no clever words. She was all clevered out.

That afternoon Mr. Garrett taught the class about the power of friendship—of all things. He said unlikely friendships sometimes made up the fabric of history.

*Unlikely friendships.* Ashley smiled at that idea.

Mr. Garrett told them, "For instance, Alexander Graham Bell is famous for inventing the telephone, but did you know that he became a close friend to Helen Keller—who could not hear or speak?" He paused. "That's not a likely friendship. Mr. Bell helped Helen Keller attend school as a result. His friendship with her had a big impact on history."

Ashley let loose a quiet sigh. She was glad Helen Keller had a friend like Mr. Bell. But what about her? Where was her unlikely friend? How come no one in this class had stepped forward to fill the spot?

Mr. Garrett walked to his desk. "We are going

to make friendship bracelets today. I want you to think about someone from our class who you wouldn't normally be friends with." He laid out the materials on the large table at the side of the room. "Maybe they play a different sport than you, or maybe you think they talk too much . . . or that their love for comic books is strange."

Their teacher made his eyes really big, and the class giggled.

"Give that person your friendship bracelet." Mr. Garrett nodded. "Take a chance and make a friend." He shrugged. "You just might change history."

Ashley was one of the last to visit the supply table. She loved what her teacher had said. Jesus had said basically the same thing in the Bible: Love one another. That's what Mr. Garrett was talking about. Being kind. Sacrificing for someone else.

But you had to have a friend before you could show kindness, right? Ashley picked out pretty pink and white threads along with a few purple ones and she set to work on her bracelet.

Even though she couldn't think of a single classmate who could wear it.

. . .

Back at the house, Ashley changed clothes and found her sketchbook and pencils. Then she made her way downstairs. She was sketching herself covered in mud—so she wouldn't forget how she felt—when she heard Mom's voice.

"Ashley." Her mother called out from the living room. "There's mail for you on the kitchen counter."

*Mail?* Ashley felt her heart do a little dance. She walked to the kitchen and there it was. She read her name across the front and then at the upper left corner she saw—

"Lydia!" Ashley screamed her old friend's name. "It's from Lydia!"

She grabbed the letter and ran to the front porch

141

swing. As soon as she was settled in, she tore open the envelope.

Ashley . . . Hello from Ann Arbor! Summer was boring without you. I did go to Camp Waterloo and I learned how to fence. It was awesome. School has been okay. Things are definitely different since you moved. How is Bloomington? Are you making friends? We should write more letters to each other. I saw Samson the other day. You know, the butterfly from last year. I told him to fly to you and say hi. Miss you, Ashley Baxter! Talk to you soon! Your best friend, Lydia.

Ashley closed her eyes and held the letter to her heart. "Thank You, God, for this happy moment," she whispered. "It was just what I needed." She folded up the letter and put it back in the envelope. Then she opened her sketchbook, and for a long time she looked again at the picture of her home in Ann Arbor.

Finally she turned to a blank page and drew an octopus. Except accidentally he had only seven legs. She giggled. Seven, eight. How could it matter? She added herself deep-sea diving with three sea turtles next to the octopus.

There. That was better.

She was halfway through another sketch when her daddy came out onto the porch. He took the chair beside her. "Sort of a muddy day, huh?"

Ashley stared at the rainy sky. "Yeah." She looked straight at her dad's eyes. "First mud, then the class menace."

"Menace?" Dad raised his brow. "I didn't hear about that."

"Landon Blake." She frowned. "He teases me all the time."

A little grin came up Dad's face, but then it dropped off. "Is the boy being mean?"

"Hmm." Ashley remembered the day. "Not mean, really. Just a menace."

"I see." Dad was quiet for a minute. "You know, Ashley, you can stand up for yourself." He paused. "But as far as this boy being a menace." Dad put his arm around Ashley and pulled her close. "Sometimes, people say the wrong things. Even if they mean well, it can come across wrong."

Ashley thought about that. "True."

"Maybe he's not a menace." Dad patted her head. "He might just need practice at being nice. Or acting his age." Dad made a silly face.

This made Ashley giggle.

"He says I'm spunky." She wrinkled her nose. "So yes, he's a menace."

Dad thought for a second. "Well . . . you've already had the mud and the menace." He pulled something from his pocket. "Now it's time for some Mentos." He handed them to Ashley.

"My favorite!" Ashley jumped up, and leaned over to hug her dad. "You always make things better. And guess what? Lydia wrote to me!"

"That's what Mom said." Dad turned to her picture. "What are you drawing?"

Ashley held it out. "This one is me . . . and the only person who could ever wear the friendship bracelet we made in school today."

"Lydia?" Dad gave her an understanding look.

"Yes." For the first time today, Ashley blinked away tears. "It had to be someone from our class. And . . . last year, she was in my class." She leaned her head on her daddy's shoulder. "But I can't give it to her, because Lydia is back home. And home is a million miles away from here."

Her dad pulled her into a safe hug, and they stayed that way for a while. Ashley stared at her Mentos. And even though that was the sad truth about Lydia, she felt a little happier.

Because Daddy understood her heart.

And that was the best news all day.

## 11

# *Adventure Day and the Green Lava*

### KARI

The rocks were getting heavier.

They filled an invisible bag and weighed against Kari's back and shoulders everywhere she went. Guilt rocks. Because she still hadn't told anyone what she'd done. How she'd cheated on the history test.

Every day at school with her new friends, Liza and Mandy, Kari could almost feel the word *cheater* written across her forehead. What would happen if the girls found out? What about Ms. Nan?

It was getting to be more than Kari could handle.

Which was why she was so happy it was Saturday morning. A day to just be with her family. Ashley had forgiven her about the swim team dilemma, and since then their biggest problem was sleep.

Because at night they always had so much to talk about.

Kari sat by the living room window and wrote in her journal. She loved Saturday mornings because time seemed to stop. Never mind the rocks, today it felt like she had forever to gather her thoughts and write about them.

"Morning." Ashley came down the stairs. She smiled at Kari. "Feels like an Adventure Day to me."

This was the sister she loved so much. "Like when we were little!"

"Right." Ashley poured herself a bowl of cereal. "Because there's no law that fifth- and sixth-grade girls can't have an Adventure Day!"

"True." Kari shut her journal. "Maybe we'll find something!"

Brooke entered the kitchen from the garage door. She was practically buried in a stack of flattened cardboard boxes. "A little help please!" She huffed, out of breath. "I need these on the big table."

Kari jumped up and grabbed three of the boxes

147

from Brooke. When they unloaded their arms, there were seven total boxes spread across the table. Kari looked at their oldest sister. "What are these for?"

"Carly is coming over." Brooke brushed her hair off her face. "We need to work on our science project!"

Kari grabbed a bowl of cereal, too. She looked at Brooke. "Last week you couldn't decide what you wanted to do."

Brooke rummaged through the kitchen drawers. "We're making a volcano."

Kari glanced at Ashley, and the two of them turned to Brooke. "Really?" Kari put her spoon down. "With lava and everything?"

"Yes! It'll win for sure!" Brooke found a roll of duct tape and began attaching the flat cardboard pieces together. After a minute she stepped back and surveyed her work. "Perfect base. Where's Mom?"

Kari nodded to the back door. "She's in the garden with Erin." Kari walked back to the couch. She flopped down and opened her journal again. She picked up where she'd left off.

Okay. I'm back . . . Cheating is especially stressful because if someone finds out, I'll be punished for sure. I'll probably have to pay a fine. Or get expelled. Or worse, maybe I'll have to tell the entire class what I did. An hour of shame! That would be horrible.

The doorbell rang. "That's Carly!" Brooke half slid, half ran to the front door. Kari closed her journal and tucked it under the couch. Because those secrets were for her and God alone.

Carly always sounded like someone was chasing her. Today was no different. She followed Brooke to the kitchen table, talking the whole way. "So, I was thinking we could use a balloon! And then maybe put some red glitter in it and I was reading about how heat can make a balloon pop." She took a breath, probably so she wouldn't pass out. "I have a million ideas. For instance there was this book I read once that . . ."

Kari tuned the girl out and joined Ashley at the kitchen counter again. They watched Brooke and

Carly bounce ideas around like Ping-Pong balls. Finally, Ashley leaned close to Kari. "I'm worried." She kept her voice to a whisper. "I hope they don't burn the house down. Lava's hot, you know."

This was what Kari loved about Ashley. She always found a way to make her laugh. "I think the house will be okay." An idea came to her. "Let's go outside and see what Mom and Erin are doing! Race you out back!"

Before Ashley could answer, Kari took off. They weren't going to have an Adventure Day sitting in the house watching Brooke and Carly. The air was cool and it smelled sweet like autumn leaves. Summer was officially winding down.

Kari breathed in deep as she ran. Fall made the morning even more exciting. Best time of the year. The trees were already turning yellow and red and they could play outside all day and never get too hot.

Kari reached the grass. "I won!" She pumped her hands in the air and then rested them on the tree.

"Not fair!" Ashley was close behind. "You cheated!"

Kari's heart nearly stopped. Why did Ashley say that? Had she read the journal? And if Ashley knew, had she told other people?

Kari spun around and looked at Ashley. "How did you know?" She could barely speak. Her whole life was collapsing around her.

Ashley tilted her head to one side and exhaled. "What"—her words came between breaths—"are you talking about?"

Kari blinked a few times. "What are *you* talking about?" Kari tried to cover her tracks. She didn't want to give herself away.

"The race. You got a head start!" Ashley put her hands on her hips. "It wasn't a fair race."

"Oh . . . yeah." Kari tried to laugh, but her voice sounded funny. "Right. I get it. I cheated." Kari couldn't quite find her smile.

"Are you okay?" Ashley looked confused.

Kari felt panic creeping in around her. She couldn't keep this secret forever. "I don't know. Forget it!" She started walking toward the garden. "We have to find our adventure!"

The garden was just off the right side of the backyard. But to get there, Kari and Ashley had to walk over a series of flat, gray stepping-stones. Kari stepped out on the first one and then she felt Ashley's hand on her shoulder.

"Wait!" Ashley yelled. She sounded superscared. "Oh, no!"

Kari's heart beat faster as she turned around. "What?"

Ashley looked like she'd seen a snake. She pointed to the grass all around them. "It's . . . it's green lava!" Ashley's breathing came faster. "We're in danger here! Stay on the stones!" She still had hold of Kari's shoulder. "Don't let it swallow you up!"

A quick turn and Kari could see it now, too. Ashley was right. Suddenly the grassy field was bubbling, melting, green soupy lava. And it made the hottest heat ever. Kari covered her face with her arm, anything to shield herself.

She looked back at Ashley. "What should we do?" Kari had to yell so Ashley could hear her over the noisy lava.

"It's rising!" Ashley yelled even louder. She took hold of Kari's hand. "You lead, but not too fast!"

"Okay!" Kari crouched down a little and focused on the journey ahead. She felt Ashley lean into her. Kari gritted her teeth. The green lava was getting hotter. "Jump to the next stone!" Kari took off and landed. Safe! She turned to her sister.

Ashley was staring at the lava. "I can't do it!" She shrank back.

"Yes, you can!" Kari shouted. She held out both hands. "Come on! Jump!"

"I might slip!" Ashley closed her eyes.

The lava was starting to swallow up Ashley's right shoe. Kari couldn't bear to watch. "Now! Hurry!" Kari pointed to her sister's foot. "The lava is catching you!" Kari was breathless.

Ashley must have noticed her hot sticky shoe. She set her eyes on the rock where Kari was and then, in an instant, she left the ground and leapt.

"You made it!" Kari put her arm around her sister. "I knew you could do it!" She jumped to the next stone. "Come on! We're running out of time!"

"I'm coming!" Ashley called back.

The girls jumped over the boiling green lava, from rock to rock. On the last one, Ashley stopped. "My toes are so hot! I can't make it!" She looked down. "The stone is crumbling!"

The lava was louder now, rising higher. Kari cupped her hands around her mouth and yelled. "I'll help you!" Using all her strength, Kari stretched her body and arms as far as she could. She grabbed Ashley's hand and yanked her to the stone.

Instead of landing safely, both girls collapsed on the grass. They were right in the middle of the bubbling green lava! Kari started to laugh. The fear left her. "Look at that." She glanced down. "It's grass again."

The worry in Ashley's eyes disappeared. "Yeah." She giggled. "Look at that."

Kari stood and helped Ashley to her feet. Then she smiled at her sister. "Glad we made it out."

"Me, too." Ashley brushed the grass off her hands and shorts. She blew a wisp of hair away from her forehead. "Thanks for saving me."

"All in a day's work." Kari shared a silly look with Ashley. "We survived another Adventure Day!"

"Yes." Ashley put both hands high in the air and danced in a small circle. "Yes, we actually did."

Mom stopped planting and called out to them. "Looked like you girls were in danger."

"We were!" Kari pointed at the grass. "The green lava river is hotter than the sun. It already swallowed up every stepping-stone." She looked from her mom to Erin and back again. "We need to find another way back to the house."

"Yes." Ashley put her hands on her hips. "And we'd advise you two to do the same." She nodded, her eyes serious. "Just looking out for the citizens of this town."

"Thank you." Mom seemed to cover up a laugh. "I didn't know the lava river was so full this time of year." She put her arm around Erin's shoulders. "Send a messenger so we know the best way home."

"Yes, ma'am!" Kari turned to Ashley. "Ready?"

Ashley saluted. "Off we go!" She ran toward the front of the house, and Kari followed.

They darted in and out of a dozen trees. They dodged a wild bear and then a hungry lion and the whole time the bubbling green lava kept spreading, sending gobs of hot goop everywhere. Kari and Ashley jumped and slid and veered and ran, barely escaping one terror after another.

Finally they made a last leap and landed on the front porch. Kari bent over and tried to steady herself.

"Whew!" Ashley wiped her forehead. "I need water!"

"Me, too." Kari grinned as they walked to the front door. "Best Adventure Day in years!"

"So fun." Ashley looked at her. "We can always have Adventure Days. Even when we're old. Like twenty or thirty."

"Yeah!" Kari giggled. "Adventures are for old people, too!"

"Kari." Ashley turned to her. Suddenly her voice got very low and serious. "Can I tell you a secret?"

"Sure . . ." Kari held her breath. Nothing was as bad as the secret she herself was keeping.

"Okay . . ." Ashley looked over one shoulder, then the other. "I don't like this house. I don't like Bloomington. I don't like our school." She was very still.

"Ashley." Kari raised her eyebrows. "I don't think that's much of a secret."

"No." Ashley shook her head. "That's not the secret part. The secret part is that I am looking for an opportunity to get back to Ann Arbor as soon as I can, and then I'm—"

"Ashley," Kari interrupted her. "Just how are you going to do that?"

"Run away, I guess." Ashley shrugged and flicked a rock off the porch. "I'll leave on a train maybe. Or I could ask Marsha's mom to take me." She hesitated. "If her baby doesn't come first."

Worry came over Kari. Her mouth hung open. Was her sister kidding? "What about food and money? And a place to live?" Kari paused. "Our old house belongs to someone else now."

"I know. I hate that." Ashley tapped her chin. "I still have some wrinkles to smooth out." Ashley paced a few steps down the length of the porch and then she stopped and put her hands on her hips. "All I know is I *don't* want to stay here." Then she walked slowly back and leaned her forehead on Kari's shoulder. "Until I find a way, I'm glad to have you."

"Me, too. I don't think you should run away." Kari and Ashley sat on the front step for a bit. The wind made a soft noise across the porch. Kari looked away, out over the open field that was their front yard. "You know, Ash"—way out at the edge of their property, a car whizzed by—"you're still my best friend. No matter how many new friends I meet. Right?"

"I know." Ashley's expression grew soft. "Same here." Then she laughed and rolled her eyes. "If I ever actually make a new friend."

"You have Marsha." Kari shrugged. "Right?"

Ashley tossed her long hair. "I never see her."

The girls helped each other to their feet and headed into the kitchen. They were laughing about Adventure Day and the green lava when they reached the kitchen.

Where they walked into a different kind of lava disaster.

Melted candle wax and glitter covered the floor and counters and kitchen table. Brooke and Carly sat side by side, frozen. Brooke stared at the ceiling. Her head lay all the way back against her chair.

Carly was hunched forward, her chin on the table.

Apparently the science project was not so simple after all.

Ashley walked up to Brooke and Carly. "Look." She studied the two defeated girls. "I know you didn't ask for my advice. But—"

"Give it!" Brooke sat straight and looked at Ashley. "We'll take what we can get."

Kari watched, curious. How could Ashley help? *This should be good,* she thought.

Ashley ran to her backpack, unzipped it, and pulled out some candy. "Mentos." She smiled. "Dad gave me these."

"What do Mentos have to do with a volcano explosion?" Brooke made a face.

"Exactly." Ashley skipped to the fridge. "I thought you'd never ask." She opened the door and rummaged around.

Kari patted Brooke on the arm. "Sorry about the kitchen."

"Thanks." Brooke sounded a little more hopeful. "We have to find a way."

Ashley returned with a can of Coke. "Ta-da."

She held it out. "Behold . . . your secret weapon!" She set the can on the table. "One Mento in this and . . . voilà! Explosion!"

"Hmmm." Brooke studied the can. "How do you know?"

"Eric from last year used to talk about this all the time." Ashley shrugged. "He said it works."

Carly lifted her chin off the table. "It's worth a try!"

"Let's see." Brooke opened the Coke can. She took one of Ashley's Mentos and plopped it inside. "Here goes."

The eruption began before Brooke finished her sentence, and without warning, the pop bubbled over.

And over and over and over!

"Wow!" Kari's jaw dropped. "It works!"

"See?" Ashley was clearly proud of herself.

But now the foamy Coke was oozing onto the table and spilling down to the floor.

Carly was the first to act. "Someone help!" She picked up the can and ran for the sink. With every step, a river of dark liquid Coke bubbled out and onto the floor. "It won't stop!"

Once the can was in the sink, the danger ended. Kari peered at it. Even now the can was erupting.

Brooke looked around. "I can't believe this." The kitchen was the worst mess ever. "I'll get the old towels from the garage!"

Kari smiled as they cleaned the mess.

One of these years she and Ashley would be old enough for their own science experiments. But for now Kari would rather have an Adventure Day with her sister. Anything to keep her from running away to Ann Arbor.

As Kari ran a towel over the kitchen table, something caught her eye. She looked outside. A green bubbly river was glowing just beyond the bushes. *Yes.* Kari smiled as she got back to work.

The green lava was still rising.

# 12

## The Cartwheel Queen

### ASHLEY

Butterflies tumbled around in Ashley's stomach. She was in the car with Mom, headed to her very first gymnastics lesson, and all her confidence about this sport was gone.

Ashley pressed her hand against her tummy and turned to her mother. "I don't feel good. This leotard is cutting off my strangulation."

Every way she twisted, to the right and left, back and front, the pink material wouldn't smooth out. What had she been thinking? Gymnastics was Marsha's sport, not hers. Ashley closed her eyes. "Mother, please go back. Turn around."

Mom glanced at her. "Your leotard is not cutting off your *circulation*. It's a little large, if anything."

She looked straight ahead. "You haven't even tried gymnastics, Ashley." She smiled. "You'll probably love it."

"Probably not. *Circulation* is a big deal." Ashley blinked her eyes open and tugged at the fabric around her shoulders. Strangulation felt more like it. And now they were almost there. "Plus, Marsha started gymnastics when she was three. It's too late for me." She paused. "Don't make me do it."

"Ash, honey." Mom kept her eyes on the road. "You'll be fine."

"I won't." Ashley crossed her arms hard. Mom didn't understand. "I can't compete with Marsha and her friends. Not in a million years. I could never be them."

Mom's voice stayed calm and patient. "Remember last year when you tried to be like Brooke?" She paused. "You stopped soccer and tried to study harder? To be like her?"

"Yes . . ." Ashley shrank back in her seat. "It wasn't my best moment."

"Right." Mom stopped at a red light and took a deep breath. "So be yourself. Gymnastics is fun. And everyone has to start somewhere."

The butterflies stopped tumbling. "True." Ashley hadn't thought of it that way. "This could just be my starting place."

"Exactly! You might turn out to be a cartwheel queen!" Mom patted Ashley's hand. She pulled up in front of the gym. "I'll be back early so I can watch you."

Mom had to pick up Brooke from middle school. Brooke was playing violin this year for the school orchestra. And Kari was at the rec center swimming. Ashley felt her confidence coming alive again. "Sounds good. Then after we can go to the house and hear how everyone's activities went!"

"*Home,* you mean?" Mom gave her a half smile and waited.

Ashley stared out the window at the gymnasium. "It's not home." Her words were quiet. Because she didn't want Mom to think she was being rude.

"Kari told me you're thinking of running away. Taking the train or . . . asking Marsha's mom to drive you." She looked straight at Ashley.

"Well . . ." Ashley swallowed hard. Kari wasn't

supposed to say anything. But at least she cared. "Maybe those were the wrong words." She folded her arms and looked out the window again. "But I am planning on returning home one day. As soon as I can."

Mom sighed. "I wish you wouldn't. We would all miss you a whole lot if you left us."

"You can always come visit." Ashley turned back to her mom and smiled.

"Oh, Ashley." Mom ran her fingers through Ashley's hair. "Please. Stop fighting against our move. Pay attention to what's happening around you. Bloomington is amazing . . ."

Ashley slumped in her seat. "I don't think so." She felt the sting of tears in her eyes. Mom didn't sit next to silent Natalie in class. And she didn't have a drafty old place for a bedroom.

"Well, let's just wait and see." Mom's voice was even kinder than before. "Have fun, Ashley! This is Day One. Remember that."

"Okay." Ashley climbed out and waved to her mom. Her mother meant well. Plus, she always had the best advice at times like this.

As Ashley walked toward the gym, she clenched her fists and closed her eyes. "You can do this, Ashley Baxter. You can do this." She exhaled and walked through the front door.

Marsha ran up and led her to a group of girls. They had pink leotards, just like Ashley. Confidence flooded over her. The leotard felt better now. Not so much strangulation.

Marsha introduced her to the girls and then Coach Beth sat them down. "I've been a gymnast most of my life," the coach said. She was old. Maybe in college. "We'll go over simple moves today, since some of you are new."

Ashley looked at the other girls. These were her new teammates. This was her team! And just like that she could feel herself choosing joy. Because it was a decision. That was the lesson last week at Sunday school. Choose joy.

A giant padded mat stretched across the gym floor. The coach directed each girl to find a spot. "Give yourself room." She smiled. "Falling is normal at first."

*Remember that,* Ashley told herself. *Falling is normal.*

First they raised their arms high, and next they touched their toes. They leaned one way and then the other. Coach Beth called it stretching.

"Now we will do a bear walk." The coach bent at her waist and balanced on her hands and feet. She walked around that way. Then she stood and pointed to them. "Your turn."

Ashley bent in half and put her hands flat on the floor. Then she walked around in circles and lines, back and forth. *Look at that!* Happiness came over her. She was very good at bear walking. Who knew?

So good that she kept walking like a bear even after Coach Beth changed activities.

"Ashley?" The coach was looking at her.

From her upside-down position, Ashley peered through her legs. She stayed on all fours, frozen. "Yes, ma'am?"

The coach's eyes got wide. "We are doing somersaults now."

"Somersaults." Ashley stood. "Yes, ma'am." Ashley looked at Marsha. Her friend was doing very perfect little rolls across the mat. Didn't look too hard. Ashley scrunched up in a ball and tucked her head under. The first time she did it, her legs flew out and crashed on the padded floor.

Ashley lay there for a short moment. But she ordered the butterflies in her stomach to stay still. "It's your first time, Ashley," she whispered to herself. "Try it again."

Four more attempts and finally Ashley got it. Tuck, push forward, roll then land on her feet. She stood and put her hands straight up. Because that's what gymnasts do.

Marsha had taught her that.

"Very good, girls." Coach Beth smiled at Ashley. "I think you're getting it."

Yes. Ashley did an invisible clap for herself. Because her mother always said humility was part of sports. But she really was getting it. Her coordination was growing.

Next came the balance beam. The coach showed them how the beam lay low along a pit of foam rubber pieces. "If you fall, it won't hurt. The pit is for soft landings."

Ashley stared at the pit. *They should have one of*

*these for fifth grade,* she thought. That's where she really needed a soft landing.

"The beam is my favorite!" Marsha took Ashley by the hand and they got in line behind four other girls. "I always feel like a graceful hummingbird. Barely touching the beam."

That sounded wonderful. Ashley could hardly wait.

It was Marsha's turn, and sure enough, Ashley's friend practically floated across the beam to the other side of the pit. So far not one gymnast had fallen.

Ashley was next. She held her breath as she stepped onto the beam. It was much skinnier than it looked from the back of the line. "You can do this," she whispered. "Just like Adventure Day. One step at a time. Stay away from the green lava."

But her feet didn't feel light on the beam. They felt heavy. Like elephant feet. *Crash! Crash!* Every step shook the beam. She was five steps out over the pit when she began to wobble.

Before she could catch herself, the wobble got

worse. "Help!" She screamed the word just as her whole body fell into the foam pit. Very quick she sat up and looked around. All the girls and Coach Beth were watching. "I'm okay." She waved them off. "I'm fine."

Ashley bounced a little. She was better than fine. This foam pit was wonderful. Way more fun than the beam. She rolled onto her back and then onto her front and bounced some more. This was nothing like the green lava back at her house.

Coach Beth walked closer. "Ashley . . ." She smiled, but it didn't reach her voice. "We don't play in the pit. Please make your way back to the mat."

"Can I try again?" Ashley hurried out of the foam rubber. "Please?"

The coach hesitated. "Sure. One more time."

Ashley still had elephant feet as she moved onto the beam. But this time she didn't care. And halfway across when she started to wobble, she did a little burst with her feet and flew into the air before her whole body fell against the foam pieces. This was like being on a trampoline. Only better.

She quickly sat up and looked at the coach. "Sorry." She couldn't admit that falling was better than walking on the beam. "Apparently I'm not very good at this activity."

"I see that." Coach Beth directed Ashley out of the pit. Then she patted Ashley's shoulder. "You'll get better."

Finally it was time for cartwheels. Ashley felt the stomach butterflies tumbling around again. If only she could remember how it felt to cartwheel across the lake. Luke had told her later that her form had been perfect that time.

The girls found their spots on the mat. Marsha gave her a thumbs-up. "You got this!"

Ashley nodded. She watched Coach Beth demonstrate a perfect cartwheel. Almost like she was a cartwheel machine.

"Okay," Ashley told herself. She put her arms straight up. "Here I go." She hurled her body to the ground, but this time was even worse than on the grass at the lake. Her arms crumpled and she fell straight down. Her face broke her fall. "Ugh." She sat up and squinted a few times. Once more she looked at Coach Beth. "I'm okay! Again! Really!"

The other girls didn't seem to notice, which was the best news.

Ashley raised her hands high again. She would get it right. She really would. A few running steps and then she threw herself to the mat. This time she landed hard on her side. *Thwap!* Her breathing wasn't quite normal for a little bit.

"Let me show you." Coach Beth walked up and helped Ashley to her feet. She put her hands firm around Ashley's arms. "Lock your elbows. Pretend your arms are pieces of wood. Then really push yourself over."

*Pieces of wood!* Yes, that would be better. Until now her arms had behaved more like pieces of spaghetti. Ashley stood and lifted her arms over her head, stiff and straight.

Before going, Coach Beth checked Ashley's elbows. "Perfect. Just like that."

Ashley took some more steps and this time when she threw herself down, her strong arms caught her! Like they were actual pieces of wood! And before she knew it, her body followed all the way around.

She had done it! A professional cartwheel on the mat!

"See!" Coach Beth clapped and gave Ashley a high five. Then she moved on to help another girl.

Ashley stood tall and raised both hands again. She had done it! And now she could picture herself getting a medal. Being the best cartwheeler in the universe. She tried it again and again, and each time her move felt better. More graceful.

Like a hummingbird.

Ashley loved this. Gymnastics was her new most favorite sport!

Especially cartwheels.

Marsha ran over and hugged her. "You did it! I knew you could."

Her breathing was fast because of so many

cartwheels in a row, so Ashley put her hands on her knees and rested. She smiled up at Marsha. "I prayed all week that I could do a cartwheel today."

Marsha smiled. "I guess it worked!"

"Yeah." Ashley had her breath back. She stood a little taller.

Marsha zipped her hoodie and pointed to the lobby. Both their moms were watching and waiting. "Let's cartwheel our way to the door."

After three cartwheels, Ashley stood and ran to her mom. "I did it!"

"I can see that!" Mom kissed the top of her head. "I've been watching!"

On their way out, Coach Beth called to Ashley. "You're going to be a very good gymnast, Ashley!" She waved at her. "See you next week."

"Thanks!" Ashley grinned at her coach and then her mother. She picked up her bag and skipped out the door. When she and her mom got back to the house, Ashley rushed to the table, pulled out her sketchbook, and started to draw. Her hand flew across the page and she giggled as she drew. She blew off the eraser shavings and surveyed her work. There. Just like she'd pictured. Herself in the pink leotard. On a podium with a medal. Then she remembered one last touch. A crown.

Because she really was a cartwheel queen, after all.

# 13

## *The Tangle*

**ASHLEY**

The octopus report turned out to be more fun than Ashley expected. So many legs and such a funny face. Definitely one of the most interesting animals ever.

Note cards with facts about the octopus lay scattered across Ashley's desk. Also the sketch she had done of the seven-legged octopus. Suddenly a question popped into her head and she shot her hand up.

"Yes, Ashley?" Mr. Garrett walked up to her. "Do you need help?"

"Okay." Ashley sent a quick look at her notes and then back to the teacher. "I was thinking how fish travel in schools and dolphins in pods." She grinned. "Something I learned in this class, by the way. Thank you for that."

Mr. Garrett laughed. "You're welcome."

She made her best curious face. "What about octopuses?" Enthusiasm filled her voice. "I'm thinking they should be called a 'tangle.'"

The other kids were working on their projects, but now most of them looked up. All except Natalie, who minded her own business. A few kids giggled.

"What?" Ashley stared at them "It's true." She turned back to Mr. Garrett. "You know, because that many octopuses with all those legs would probably become a giant tangle in no time. Especially after a game of kickball or something. Whew! What a mess."

Her teacher pushed his lips together. Like he was trying hard to be serious. "Actually, there is no name for a group of octopuses. They are solitary creatures, usually found by themselves."

Ashley blinked. "Oh. So not a tangle." She felt the wind leave her sails as she erased *Tangle* from her note card. "Okay." She could still feel her classmates watching. *Stop staring,* she wanted to say. *Nothing to see here.*

Gradually the other kids returned to their work and Ashley focused on her notes. No wonder Mr. Garrett had assigned her the octopus.

Besides Natalie, Ashley was the most solitary creature in fifth grade.


School was almost over and Ashley was returning a bottle of glue to the art station when Elliot walked up. "Ashley." He was chewing a really big piece of gum. "Take me to your leader!" He held his hands out and made a clicking sound with his mouth, like he had so often.

Sometimes Elliot left her speechless. "I have no words, Elliot." She couldn't stop staring at his gum.

Elliot had braces, so the gum sort of dangled near his lips while he chewed it. An idea hit her. "Actually I have a word. One of our spelling words for the week." Ashley stood a little straighter. "Anomaly." She nodded. "That's my word for you, Elliot."

"Something different from the normal and expected! Anomaly." He grinned. "I love this week's words." He raised his pointer finger. "And you know what? This one time"—he slid his glasses up closer to his eyes—"I got a squid from a fishing store and it inked all over me. Which was also an anomaly." His eyes got wide. "Because I really liked that squid."

Why would he tell her that? Ashley made a face. "Sounds messy."

"It was. But in the greatest way." His gum almost fell out of his mouth, but he caught it and shoved it back in.

"You know, Elliot, you really shouldn't be chewing gum in class. It's not allowed. If Mr. Garrett saw, you'd be in big trouble." Ashley looked at the wad of gum that Elliot worked through his teeth.

"He doesn't care." Elliot rolled his eyes. "I never get in trouble for chewing gum."

At this point, Ashley was desperate to get back to her desk. "So . . . hey, I gotta go."

"Wait." Elliot stepped in front of her. "I have a model spaceship at home. Did you know that?"

Ashley sighed. Where was this going? "That's nice." She waited. Maybe if she gave him some time he would make a point. Patience was a good skill, after all.

"Okay, well . . ." He laughed and the sound turned into a snort. "Bye, Ashley!" His wave was a little too aggressive. "Hope the rest of your day is perfect!"

But as Elliot said the word *perfect* the most terrible thing happened. His huge piece of slippery pink gum came barreling out of his mouth and— almost in slow motion—landed deep in Ashley's hair. Just below her ear.

"Oh no." Elliot's face looked suddenly pale. "I'm sorry. I'll get it."

"That's okay!" Ashley tried to back up, but it was too late. In a flash Elliot grabbed at the gum, but then his face looked even more concerned. "It's . . . it's stuck."

Ashley reached to feel it and her heart skipped a beat. His sticky wet germy gum was matted up in her hair from her ear to her chin. "I . . . I don't know what to say." She backed away. Her knees and heart were shaking.

Real quick Elliot grabbed his backpack and started digging around. "Here!" He pulled out a pair of scissors. "I'll cut it out!"

*Of all things.* "No!" Ashley stopped him. "I'm fine. You've . . . you've done enough."

"Sorry, Ashley. Really." Elliot looked terrible. Like he might lose his lunch. As the bell rang, he sprinted out of the classroom.

Ashley still stood there. What was she supposed to do? She didn't see Landon Blake until he was standing right in front of her.

"Hi, Ashley." He held up a photo of a sea turtle. "I wanted to show you how—"

"I have to go." She whipped around before he could see the gum in her hair. She raised her hand in a miniwave without looking back. "Goodbye." She grabbed her backpack and hurried into the hall.

Landon caught her. "Hey!" He jogged to keep up. "Why are you going so fast?"

Ashley held her hand along the side of her face. "My mom's waiting." He absolutely couldn't see the gum in her hair. *Please, God, don't let him see it.*

But Landon stayed beside her. "I just wanted to show you . . ." He took hold of her hand and lowered it.

"Don't." Ashley jerked her hand back. She stopped walking and faced him. "If I wanted you to see me I'd—"

Before she could finish, Landon did a sudden gasp. "Ashley." He pointed to the gum side of her hair. "You . . . you have . . ."

"I know." Ashley folded her arms and stared at Landon. "I don't exactly want the whole world to see this newest bad situation. Someone accidentally . . ." She paused. "You know what? It doesn't matter."

"It was Elliot! I saw him talking to you." Landon brought his hand to her hair and then changed his mind. "You're not going to get that out."

"Thank you." Ashley gave him a look. "I sort of figured that."

Landon studied her. "But you'll still look pretty with short hair. So don't worry."

"Short hair!" Never mind the part about being pretty. Now she was really angry. "For your information, I've always had long hair. A piece of gum doesn't mean short hair!"

The expression on Landon's face told her he had his doubts. "Okay." He couldn't take his eyes off the smashed gum. A smile came up his face. He looked right at her. "I will say . . . now that's a *tangle*."

Ashley stared at him. "You think you're so funny, Landon."

"Actually"—he chuckled—"I think *you're* so funny."

Something about the way he said that made Ashley laugh, too.

They reached the front steps of the school and Ashley saw her mom waiting in the van. She didn't want another person to spot her hair crisis. "I have to go." Another giggle came from her. Because that tangle line really was funny.

"Okay. See ya, Ashley." Landon turned and walked down the sidewalk toward the buses.

*How could someone be both annoying and funny at the same time?* She might have to process that one later. Two more boys from her class were walking her way. Ashley raced for the van. The second she was buckled in, she slammed the door and turned to her mom. "Go! Please, Mom." Panic pounded in Ashley's heart. "Drive!"

"Hello to you, too." Mom sounded caught off guard. "What's wrong? We need to wait for your siblings."

Ashley flipped down the visor and stared at herself. "I can't wait." The longest whimper came from her. "I'm destroyed again. Ruined." She turned to her mother. "Look at me!"

"Ashley!" Mom stared at her. Disbelief colored her eyes. "I . . . I've never *seen* so much gum."

Ashley's hands came up over her face and stayed there. "I know." Her words came muffled through the cracks between her fingers. "I need a bag." She peered over her fingertips. "For my head." She blinked. "And I hate scissors near my face. As you know, Mother. From past experience."

Kari and Erin and Luke made it to the van so finally they could drive away. The other three were too busy talking to notice the gum disaster.

Mom had definitely not recovered from the gum hair news. Her eyes had a glazed look of shock. Which was saying something, because her mother didn't get shocked easily. Not with Ashley, anyway.

She dropped the other kids off and she turned to Ashley. "I'll ask Brooke to be in charge."

Ashley waited, her fingers covering the sticky mess. First Kari with the hairbrush, and now this. What was it about long hair? When Mom came back to the van, she stared at Ashley. "What happened to you?"

This was an awful situation. "I'm in a not funny television comedy." Ashley closed her eyes for a few seconds. "The most perplexing situation. My show is about a boy spitting gum straight into my hair. And I don't know what to do about it."

A small laugh came from her mother. "You mean you're in a *quandary*?"

Ashley sighed. She still couldn't get all her spelling

words right. "That's what I meant. Quandary." She peeked at her mom. "It's our spelling word today. Comedy . . . quandary. Whatever." She remembered Landon's comment about her hair being a tangle. "Actually, Mother, in this case, I think comedy maybe works, too."

Her mom bit her lip. "Sweetheart. It doesn't look *that* bad." She glanced over. "We'll get it out."

"How?" Ashley held the tangled-up hair in the air. "How are you going to get this out?"

Mom cleared her throat. "I'll take you to the hairdresser. She might have a few tricks." She paused. "If nothing else, she can cut it out."

Ashley patted her mom's hand. "Mother. Scissors next to my head is a very uncomfortable and scary moment."

"Not if you sit still." Mom drove the van toward town again. "But let's ask her to try some other things."

Mom parked the car at the hair place and looked again at the matted gum spot. "Poor girl."

Mom was right. Ashley covered her face again. This was the poorest day of fifth grade. Even worse than her famous mud day disaster. They had barely sat down when a girl in a white coat called her name.

"Ashley Baxter?" The girl seemed to be in high school. And she had spiky hair, which wasn't a very confident sign of Ashley keeping hers long.

"Give her a chance," Mom whispered to her. "It's her job to help people."

"Hmm." That sounded nice. Ashley could feel her hands shaking, but maybe if she thought about the hair-cutter girl as being helpful, this would go better.

With one hand covering her gum hair, Ashley walked with the girl back to a spinny chair. She sat down, her hand still in place. "Hello." Her smile felt as shaky as her arms and legs. "I need special help today."

"Perfect." The hairdresser lady grinned. "I'm Amber." She looked at Ashley's hand, still covering the gum situation. "Is . . . something wrong with your hair?"

"Yes." With no option left, Ashley moved her hand, and after a few seconds she dared to look at herself.

The massive mess seemed to have doubled in size since the last time she looked. "Gum was fired into my hair from someone's mouth. And now . . ." She held up the ends of that chunk. "Now this."

"Hmm." Amber studied the problem. "Someone was chewing that much gum?"

"You have to know the kid." Ashley sank back in the chair.

"Well . . . let's see what we can do." Amber draped a plastic cloak over Ashley.

Mom stood nearby. "I was thinking maybe peanut butter. Or ice."

"Exactly." Amber smiled. "I keep some around for this very reason." She stepped away. "I'll be right back."

Apparently Ashley wasn't the only girl to have a gum disaster. But after ten minutes of trying ice and peanut butter in that order, Ashley was only cold and wet and messy.

"Well. We might have to try scissors," Amber said. "I'll only cut a little."

Ashley's mother came closer and put her hand on Ashley's shoulder. "It'll be okay."

No, it wouldn't. But Ashley didn't say the words. What choice did she have? All she could do was watch Amber comb all her good hair to one side. Every piece that wasn't matted with gum.

The hair-cutter girl stepped back and did a thinking-type frown. "This is tricky."

*Exactly,* Ashley wanted to say. But she stayed quiet so Amber could figure out how to fix it.

"I can cut the gum out." The girl touched the matted side of Ashley's hair. She looked up. "But once I blend everything, your hair will be a lot shorter."

Mom looked at Amber. "How short will it have to be?"

Amber put her hand near the base of Ashley's neck. "About like this."

"Okay . . ." Mom shook her head. "Whatever you have to do. Just get it out."

"Excuse me." Ashley raised her finger. "I'd like to keep my hair long. Thank you."

The girl did a sad smile. "I understand, sweetie." She combed Ashley's good side again. "You have the most beautiful hair."

189

In the end, it didn't matter if Amber was sad about cutting Ashley's hair or if Mom was still in shock. The germy, sticky gum had to go. So that meant her hair had to go, too. Ashley closed her eyes tight so she wouldn't be witness to the terrible tragedy of seeing her hair fall to the ground.

A snip here, a snip there. Snip, snip, snip. Ashley kept her eyes closed through the whole thing. One side benefit was not seeing the scissors. It took away all her fear of being cut.

"You're doing great . . ." Amber's voice sounded calm.

"Thank you." Ashley could feel cold air against her shoulders where hair was supposed to be. "I'm really trying to be a good sport."

Another minute of snipping and then Ashley felt the scissors stop.

"Okay . . . it's done." Amber sounded hopeful. "The gum is all gone."

Ashley opened just one eyeball and looked in the mirror. She took a deep breath and opened the other one. Near her face, her hair was chopped just below her ears. It got a few inches longer toward the back of her neck. Ashley stared at the girl in the mirror. Was that really her?

The hair-cutter girl seemed proud of her work. "I'd say . . . you look like a French model. Very fashion forward."

"Thank you." Ashley stood and nodded at the girl. Before Mom could say anything, Ashley ran into her arms. "It's . . . kinda short!"

"Not really." Mom put her hands on Ashley's shoulders and looked her over. "You're so pretty, Ashley. Shorter hair makes your face that much more beautiful."

It was the number one compliment Ashley had ever gotten. *Choose joy,* she told herself. *Have an attitude of gratitude. You can do it.* Ashley felt determination filling her. She grabbed a deep breath and gave her mom a minigrin. "Maybe we won't need a bag, after all."

Her mom laughed out loud. "No. I think not."

Back at the house, Brooke was helping Kari peel potatoes when Ashley and Mom walked in. Brooke stood still and studied her. Like she was looking at a painting in a museum. "It doesn't look too bad, Ashley." She nudged Kari. "Right?"

"Yeah." Kari dried her hands and came closer. "Just a little . . . different."

"What's that supposed to mean?" Ashley didn't like what was happening here.

Just then Luke came in from outside. He put the brakes on as soon as he saw Ashley. "Whoa." He shuffled a few steps closer. His eyes grew wide, like he was seeing a real-life dinosaur. "Why'd you cut your hair off, Ash?"

"That's it." The sun hadn't set, so Ashley ran out the door, down the porch stairs, all the way through the yard to the very back. Where the rock sat against the stream. She climbed up and plopped down in the middle. And only then did she give her tears permission to escape.

"Why did he have to spit the gum at *me*?" She said the words to the sky, for God to hear. But there was no answer. Ashley worked her fingers through her hair. She missed how long it used to be.

After a few minutes her tears stopped and an

afternoon breeze dried her cheeks. She was sitting right next to the word *BAXTER* that Brooke had painted on the rock. Ashley traced it. Just maybe she had overreacted back at the house.

But why couldn't her siblings say a compliment like Mom did? No one wanted to look *different*. Just then, Ashley saw the most amazing thing. Fluttering a few feet away from her was a black and orange butterfly. Ashley wiped her nose and stood. "Samson . . . ?" She pulled the sleeves of her sweater down and bunched them in her hands, tiptoeing over to the butterfly.

Ashley was certain it was him. He must have listened to Lydia, and now he had come to say hello to Ashley. So she would know her hair looked nice. His wings fluttered a few times and then he took off, and flew up, up and away. "Take me with you," Ashley called out as the butterfly disappeared beyond the trees.

She heard a noise behind her, and a few seconds later, Brooke and Kari appeared.

"Hey." Kari climbed up on the rock and sat beside Ashley. "I'm really sorry."

Brooke followed and moved to Ashley's other

side. "We didn't mean to hurt your feelings. I like your hair. I really do!"

Ashley sniffed. "You said it looked *different*."

"Well . . . it does." Brooke let out a friendly laugh. "I'd be lying if I said it didn't." She put her arm around Ashley. "But it also looks great."

"It's the new you, Ash!" Kari bumped shoulders with her. "You look like an actress."

Ashley's heart was starting to feel better. "You mean it?"

"Definitely." Kari nodded. "I'm sorry again."

"I forgive you." Ashley exhaled long and slow. "I mean . . . who spits gum in someone's hair?" She shrugged. "Anyway, he didn't mean it. He tries to be nice." She giggled. "He keeps asking me to take him to my leader." She shrugged. "Whatever that means."

All the girls laughed and together they left the tree clearing. Hand in hand they walked back to the house, talking about Elliot and the gum tangle and Ashley's new look.

Ashley told them about Samson coming to see her at just the right time. And Kari and Brooke both thought that was nice. Ashley smiled at them. She liked having these sisters. And Erin and Luke weren't bad, either.

That night she did a sketch of herself with short hair. Also a pile of her old wonderful hair caught in a mess of gum on the floor beside her. Ashley studied the drawing. Maybe her class would think she was a different new girl and overnight she'd have all kinds of friends. And maybe they'd love her short hair—even Landon Blake. Of course, if that happened she would have Elliot to thank.

Him and his giant piece of chewing gum and the biggest tangle ever.

# 14

# The Broken Arm

## KARI

The school's first swim meet was nearly finished. Kari stood second in a row of four girls ready for the last event. The relay. The contest was at the rec center's indoor pool, but right now the whole place felt freezing cold.

Kari wiggled her chilly toes against the wet cement. Her coach's words filled her head. The second spot in a relay is very important. Never look at the swimmers on your right or left. Just go as fast as you can and pace yourself. Don't forget to breathe.

"Last is the freestyle relay." The announcer paused. "Six teams will compete in this event. Including the cheater of the year, Kari Baxter."

Kari jerked her head toward the announcer's stand. Was he really calling her out in front of everyone? She squinted, focusing on the people at the table. How did they know what she had done?

"Kari!" Liza's voice was sharp and loud. "Are you listening to me? I've been calling your name!"

Kari blinked a few times and turned to her friend. This time Liza had the right to be bossy. They were about to swim, after all. "Sorry!" Kari did a slight shake of her head. Now she was imagining voices. Great.

"We gotta stay focused!" Liza turned to the others. "Okay, everyone. Let's huddle."

They put their arms around each other and formed a small circle. Liza spoke straight at them. "We can do this! We're going to win." Confidence filled her voice. "Everyone just do your best!"

A few seconds later the announcer asked the first swimmers to take their marks and Kari watched to see if he would mention her cheating again. Or maybe that had been her imagination. The pressure of the secret and the rocks of guilt weighed on her more every day.

No one said anything else about her being a cheater.

Liza got in position. The gun went off and she dove into the pool alongside the other swimmers. All of them raced for the far wall.

Kari tightened her goggles. It was time for her to take her mark. Already Liza had hit the wall and she was swimming back. Kari took a deep breath. *Calm,* she told herself. *Stay calm.* She crouched down. She wanted to win this relay. It would keep her from thinking about being a cheater. At least for a few days.

The swimmers were getting closer. Liza was in second place and catching up.

When her friend slapped the wall, Kari dove into the pool and began to swim. *The second spot is very important.* Kari kicked like she'd never kicked before. She felt like a dolphin, gliding through the water. *Never look to the right or left . . . go fast . . . pace yourself.*

Kari hit the wall and did a somersault turn like Coach Miller had taught them. Faster and faster.

Muffled echoes of cheers and shouts from the stands hummed in her ears. What was the last thing?

Her arms sliced through the pool and she kicked still faster. Water rushed by as she kept her head down, blowing bubbles as she swam. Her heart pounded in her chest and her legs started to feel heavy. What was that last thing the coach said? Then she remembered.

*Breathe!*

That was it. The last thing was to take a breath. Kari tilted her head to one side and gasped a quick breath. Air was just what she needed. She gave a burst of effort and focused on the wall in front of her. Closer and closer and . . . *SLAP*. She hit it.

She tore off her goggles and concentrated on catching her breath. Already the next swimmer, a girl named Cheryl, was blazing hard for the other wall. Cheryl was new to their relay team. Kari lifted herself up and out of the pool. As she did, she spotted something in the crowd.

Brooke, Luke, and Erin were holding a sign that

read, WE LOVE YOU, KARI! Dad whistled and threw her a big thumbs-up, and Mom did the same. Kari's whole family was here! Ashley cupped her hands to her mouth. "Yay, Kari! You're the greatest!"

Kari grinned and waved. She had the best family ever.

Last into the pool was Mandy. Kari turned her attention back to the race as her friend flew through the water. The victory was riding on her. And suddenly Mandy swam her way into first place. Kari and Liza and Cheryl jumped and shouted, and Coach Miller joined them.

The girls clapped and cheered as Mandy's arms moved like a windmill. Her feet were kicking so fast they looked like actual flippers. Seconds later, ahead of all the other swimmers, Mandy smacked her hand against the wall.

"We did it!" Kari shouted. They waited for Mandy to join them, then they circled up again, still bouncing and yelling.

They had won their very first meet!

As they celebrated, a thought occurred to Kari. This was the right way to win. Cheating her way to an A on that history quiz was wrong, and she needed to do something about it. Needed to say something. Soon.

Yes, she might get kicked out of school or grounded for a year. Her family might never think of her the same way again. But that didn't matter.

She'd been carrying the rocks around too long.

Kari's relay team made plans to spend the night at her house, and Kari could hardly wait. Cheryl was busy with a family wedding, but Mandy and Liza would be there any minute. So, Kari decided this wasn't the night to tell her parents about her cheating. The crime was pressing in, hurting her heart. But she couldn't come clean today. Bad news only made happy days sad. And Kari didn't want anything sad.

Not after their win.

But she would tell them soon. For sure.

Just before the girls arrived, Kari and Ashley helped Mom set up the food. Dad was outside grilling burgers. Ashley opened a bag of chips and poured them into a wooden bowl. "I'm still amazed." She smiled at Kari. "You were like a pro swimmer out there!"

"Yes." Mom found her cutting board and started chopping tomatoes and onions. "You were terrific, Kari!"

"Thanks! I can't believe we won." She stirred the chip dip. "I was so nervous."

Ashley smiled. "You looked as brave as Wonder Woman."

"Hardly." Kari laughed. "I can't wait to see you on the gymnastics floor!"

Dad brought the cooked burgers inside and set them on the counter. "These are going to be good!" He grinned at Kari. "Anything for the champions."

Mom came over and put her arms around Dad's waist. "Girls"—she grinned—"your father is a pro too." Then she kissed his cheek.

At the same time the doorbell rang and Kari jumped. "I'll get it!" She raced down the hall to the front door. Liza and Mandy stood there with their sleeping bags.

"We got here at the same time!" Mandy laughed. She adjusted her glasses.

"Yay!" Kari and her friends squealed a little. Kari helped them in and shut the door behind them. "This is going to be so fun!"

When they reached the kitchen, Kari introduced the girls to her family. After Mom said hello, she stepped into the pantry for something.

Kari followed her. "Hey, Mom." Kari hugged her mother. "Can you believe it? My new friends are actually here! This is the best!" She looked into her mother's warm eyes. "Thanks. For letting them spend the night. You're the nicest mom ever."

"I like when you have friends over." Her mother kissed the top of Kari's head. "That's the sort of house your dad and I always want to have. And a good girl like you deserves to have fun nights like this one."

That's when Kari remembered her awful secret. Her smile faded as she walked back into the kitchen. If Mom knew who Kari really was, she wouldn't have said that. Cheaters shouldn't have friends over.

Now was not the time to get emotional. She had a fun night ahead of her. Kari forced a smile and joined her friends. They were eating chips and talking to Ashley.

But before Kari could help her mom with the baked beans, Brooke and Erin ran in through the back door. Their faces were pale and their eyes looked panicked. "Someone help!" Brooke cried out. "Luke fell from the tree!"

"What?" Mom dropped the bean spoon, and ran to the door. "Is he okay?"

Brooke was breathing fast. "I think . . ." She tapped her elbow. "I think it's his arm."

Mom rushed out the door with Dad. Brooke and Erin stayed inside. Kari felt sick. She looked at her friends and then at Ashley. Her sister's face was white as paper. "You okay?" Kari put her hand on Ashley's shoulder.

"I'm scared." Ashley kept her eyes on the door. "Luke's so little." She blinked, still staring across the room. "He may be tough, but he's small. I should have been out there."

Kari leaned over and hugged her sister's

shoulders. "Why was Luke climbing that old tree anyway? Dad told him not to."

Seconds later, Dad and Mom rushed back inside. Dad was carrying Luke, who had tears running down his cheeks. He was making fast gasping sounds, like he was trying to be strong.

"It's broken." Dad gave the rest of them a certain look. He glanced down at Luke. "Hang in there, buddy." Dad grabbed his keys, set Luke back on his feet, and with slow steps the two walked toward the garage door. "I'm gonna take him in." He turned back to the girls. "Mom will stay here."

Mom looked like she wanted to go, too. "Luke, you're being so brave. I'll pray for you from here. Can you find a phone when you get there? Give me an update?"

Dad nodded. "Of course."

Kari thought her mom might cry, too. She stooped down to Luke's level. "It'll be okay, honey. We'll be praying." She held his good hand. "God is with you, Luke. And Daddy, too. You won't ever be alone."

Dad and Luke left in a hurry and a few moments

of silence followed while Kari's mom stood at the door, her head bowed. Then she faced the girls. "He's going to be fine." She sat at the table with them. "He'll probably need a cast. That's all." She looked at the food spread out on the counter. "We might as well eat."

"I'm not hungry." Ashley sat back in her chair. "Not anymore."

Kari and Brooke and Erin weren't, either.

But it was awkward with Kari's friends there. This should have been a fun night with Mandy and Liza, and now Luke's broken arm had ruined everything. Of course, it wasn't his fault. Kari stared at the floor. Then she looked straight into her mother's eyes. She wanted to ask what they were they going to do now.

Mom sighed. She seemed to have more control. A quick search through two drawers and she found a stack of paper plates. "No one has to eat." She put the plates by the burgers. "But I think we'd all feel better if we did."

Kari wasn't sure what else to do. So she took a plate and a burger from the counter. The other girls did the same, and the group followed Mom back to the kitchen table.

As they sat down, Mom looked around at each of them. "Let's pray."

Kari's friends nodded. Liza folded her hands together. "We pray at my house, too."

"Interesting." Mandy shrugged. She smiled at Kari. "I like the idea."

"Great. Okay, then." Mom smiled and closed her eyes. "Father, thank You for our food, and thank You for our new friends." Her tone grew more concerned. "Please comfort Luke as he heads to the hospital. Be with the doctor who is working on him, and help him heal completely. In Jesus' name, amen."

They opened their eyes and Mandy grinned at Kari's mother. "That's it? That's praying? Just talking to God?"

"Exactly." Ashley picked up her fork. "I talk to Him all the time! Because I'm a quandary." She winked at their mother. "Right, Mom?"

"Yes." Their mother's smile looked a little softer. "Often, you are. In all the best ways, Ashley." She took a long breath. All the girls were looking at her. "So . . . I broke a bone once." The memory seemed fresh for Mom. "I was trying to impress a boy at school. We were on the swings, going superhigh and jumping off." She shook her head. "We wanted to see who could land the farthest out."

"So . . . you jumped?" Brooke leaned in, clearly surprised.

"Oh yeah. I flew off that swing, but I landed wrong. Broke my ankle." Mom made a face, like she could feel the pain again. Then she laughed.

Kari was confused. "Why is that funny?" A broken bone didn't seem like something happy.

"Because I must've looked silly. Trying so hard to get his attention." Mom took a drink of water. "I ended up limping off the playground with the school nurse." Mom sighed.

"That does sound kinda silly." Erin giggled from the other end of the table. "All because of a boy."

"I know! Exactly." Mom shrugged one shoulder. "I still can't believe I did that."

Mandy finished a bite of her burger. "One time, I was running at recess in the rain and I slipped on the grass. In front of the whole third grade." She made a funny face. "I didn't get hurt, but I landed on my back." She laughed at her old self.

Liza patted Mandy on the shoulder. "It's okay, Mandy. It wasn't the first time you embarrassed yourself."

"Probably won't be the last!" Mandy burst out laughing.

Kari was impressed by Mandy's confidence, how she was able to laugh at herself.

"You sound like me." Ashley had her color back from when Luke got hurt. She giggled. "I fell in the muddiest puddle just a few weeks ago." She stood and did a slow twirl. "I had to wear mud clothes the whole day."

Pretty soon the mood was lighter and everyone was sharing stories and laughing. Everyone except Kari. Suddenly she felt uncomfortable. She hated lying about her cheating, especially when this time together was so fun. Her shoulders sank. This was fun she didn't deserve. And tonight she couldn't shake off the truth. She was a cheater and a liar.

Which was terrible.

"So . . ." Mom turned her attention to Brooke. "How are your classes going?"

Brooke ate a single potato chip and nodded, talking as she chewed. "Great. All A's."

Mom winked. "Wonderful, honey."

"What can I say?" Brooke shrugged. "Baxters get A's. Right?" She looked around the table.

"Us, too." Liza spoke up. "Everyone in my family gets A's. I'm planning on attending an Ivy League school." She took a big bite of her burger, obviously satisfied with herself.

"Well . . ." Mom let out a small chuckle. "I'm sure you will, Liza."

Kari sank a little deeper in her chair. But before anyone could ask about her classwork, the phone rang. Mom jumped up to get it and a minute later she returned with a smile on her face. "That was Dad. Luke is going to be fine. He's getting a cast, and he's actually excited about it!" She sat back down. "The break isn't too serious, so it should heal quickly."

"Hey!" Mandy's eyes lit up. "Just like you prayed!"

"Yes." Mom sat back down at the table. "God doesn't always answer our prayers the way we want. But He always listens and He always helps us. Like He did for Luke."

Relief came over everyone. The conversation shifted to the girls' swim meet and Kari felt herself relax. Her cheating wasn't going to come up tonight.

The attention would be on her brother.

Which it was, especially after Luke came home. They all signed his cast, and Luke even joined them to make brownies and play charades.

When they headed upstairs, Kari spread her sleeping bag next to Liza's and Mandy's. Ashley stayed in her bed and for a while the girls whispered and giggled in the dark. But after they all fell asleep, Kari lay awake, staring at the ceiling.

Her mother's broken bone story made Kari realize something. She had cheated because everyone expected Kari Baxter to get an A. She was trying to impress people. Trying to keep up her image.

But Kari knew cheating was definitely wrong. And holding on to the secret of it had only made her feel worse. The guilty rocks were heavy and awful. Which meant it really was time to come clean. Even if her whole world fell apart.

The simple truth filled her heart: Kari Baxter wasn't a cheater. She didn't want to be known for getting A's if it meant stealing someone else's answers. No, Kari wanted to be known for being honest. More than anything.

Even more than getting an A.

# 15

## *Unlikely Friends*

### ASHLEY

Ashley no longer believed in boring Mondays.

She smiled about this truth as she stepped into her classroom the day after the busy weekend. Her time with her family yesterday after church had changed her view.

Dad had asked the kids to talk about their favorite day of the week. All of them said Saturday except Ashley. Her answer was Friday, "because every minute of the weekend is just ahead."

Their mom chose Wednesday, the day she and her new friends from church got together for lunch each week.

But then their dad said something different. "I

don't have a favorite." He took his time. Love was always in her daddy's eyes. "I like every day the same because each one is a unique gift from God." He smiled. "It's up to us to open it and make it the best possible day. We should expect something special everytime we wake up."

What a thought. Ashley had never pictured it that way.

So now that it was Monday, she was certain something special was going to happen.

This was Luke's first day at school since breaking his arm, and her first day with her new fashion forward haircut. That was the right term, Ashley was sure. Because the hair-cutter girl had said so. And something else was good about today . . .

This was the day she was going to look for her unlikely friend.

She was out of time for being stubborn about this topic. If she couldn't make friends with Natalie, then she needed to try another approach. Look for someone unlikely. The way Mr. Garrett said.

As it turned out, the first person to talk to her that morning was definitely unlikely. Elliot the gum boy walked right up to her. "Hello, Ashley." He wasn't chewing gum. "So . . . uh . . . your hair looks nice." He shrugged several times and his cheeks grew red. "It was my fault, the whole thing with the . . ." He looked both ways and swallowed hard. "You know . . . the—" He couldn't say the word, "gum." He seemed on the verge of a meltdown. "I'm really sorry again. I . . . waited all weekend to tell you."

Ashley raised one eyebrow. "Elliot . . . do you want to be my friend?"

His eyes lit up like Christmas. "Yes!" His braces always made it hard to say the letter *s*. So he did a few quick nods. "You're already my best friend in fifth grade."

*What?* For a few seconds Ashley didn't move. *She was Elliot's best friend?* A melting feeling warmed across Ashley's heart. "Really?" How come she hadn't known this? "I . . . I didn't think I had any friends in this class."

Elliot grinned and his braces caught the reflection of the overhead lights. "You have me, Ashley." His smile faded a little. "But . . . the gum in your hair . . ."

He hung his head. "I didn't know if you'd still want to be friends after that."

Her entire mind was spinning. All this time Elliot thought Ashley was his best friend? It was mind-gobbling. Ashley patted his shoulder. "Is that why you're always talking to me about aliens and asking me to take you to my leader?" She was seeing Elliot in a new light. Blue, maybe. For friendship. "Because I'm your friend?"

Again Elliot nodded. Then he twisted up his face in a giant question mark. "Is that okay? Can you still be my friend?"

Everything about Elliot changed in a single moment. He was no longer different and annoying and a bother. He wanted to be her friend. So maybe she had just looked at him the wrong way at first. And then because of the gum and all, well . . . But now she saw the truth.

Ashley reached out and shook his hand. "I am officially your friend, Elliot." She smiled at him. "Glad we got that figured out."

The kid had hesitation in his eyes. "But . . . the gum?"

Ashley tossed her hair. "You gave me a fashion forward haircut, Elliot. You actually helped me." She giggled. "Which is what friends do. Right?"

Relief lifted Elliot's expression. "Right!" He held up his arms. "Glad to help."

Amazement filled Ashley as they took their seats. The morning bell had just rung and already Monday was the greatest gift. Because she had done the impossible. She had made a friend in Mr. Garrett's class!

An unlikely friend. Which was her goal for today!

Their teacher moved to the front of the room. "All right, boys and girls. Quiet down. Today begins our book report week." He smiled like this was the best news. "For these reports, you'll all work with a partner."

For a long moment, Ashley refused to let her thoughts take the wrong road. She would rather draw than read, but her dad's words came back to her. *It's up to us.* The choice to enjoy this book report was hers. She sat a little straighter.

Maybe the book would make her laugh or learn

something. Maybe it would be the best book ever. Yes, that was the right way to think. Suddenly she could hardly wait. Even if she had to remind herself of that important fact every few pages.

Mr. Garrett was telling them that this time their report would be a project. "Write a poem, or make up a song. Create puppets based on the characters, or a poster board with a scene from the book." He was definitely making the most of this. "It's totally up to you."

Ashley raised her hand.

This seemed to surprise Mr. Garrett. Maybe because he was still talking. He looked at her. "Yes, Ashley?"

"Hello." She stood and smoothed out her dress. It was the green one Kari had worn last year. Ashley lifted her chin up a bit. "I'd like to compliment you on having a superexcellent attitude toward book reports this Monday morning." She smiled and gave a slight nod. "That's all."

Her teacher looked at her for a few seconds, and a smile tried to crawl up his cheeks. But then he nodded back at her. "Thank you, Ashley. I appreciate that." A quiet chuckle came from him. "And thanks for your great attitude, too."

Ashley curtsied. "You're welcome." Then she sat down.

A few of the students were watching her, so Ashley nodded her thanks to them, too. Perhaps they liked her curtsy, something Brooke had taught her over the weekend. A curtsy was a mix between a bow and a dance move. That's what Brooke said.

It had seemed like the right time for one.

Mr. Garrett passed out the books, and on Ashley's desk he set a copy of *The Mouse and the Motorcycle*. The cover was bright and fun. A cute furry mouse sat on top of a shiny red motorcycle. Then something caught her eye. Next to her, Natalie had the exact same book!

"Hey! We have the same one." Ashley leaned over to compare the two. "See?"

"I know." Natalie made a face. Now it was her turn to raise her hand. "Mr. Garrett? Did you mean to give me and Ashley Baxter the same one?"

He was still finishing handing out books. "Yes, Natalie." He walked toward the girls. "I handed out two of every book. You and Ashley are partners."

Their teacher kept talking, but Ashley couldn't quite hear him. She was paired up with Natalie? The rude girl who had ignored her every day? Ashley closed her eyes. *This is a good day. It's up to me.* She took a deep breath and reminded herself of this three times more before she looked at Natalie. Her brain raced ahead. Maybe if she forgave Natalie. That would be a good start.

So Ashley turned to the unfriendly girl. "Let's start this process right." She remembered to smile. "I forgive you for every time you were mean to me since school started." She held out her hand. "There."

But Ashley's hand just hung straight out.

Natalie wrinkled her nose at Ashley and then she glared at her hand. "I don't have to shake." She played with her long hair. "You can't make me."

"If I'm honest here"—Ashley wasn't giving up—"you do have to shake, actually. Because I *forgive* you. So, a shake seals the deal." This was harder than it looked. "We can't be partners until the air is clean here." She waited. "See . . . because right now it's still cloudy."

220

"Clear." Natalie rolled her eyes a bit. "Until the air is clear. That's how you say it."

Ashley's hand was getting tired hanging in the air. "Clear. Clean." She shrugged. "Whatever. The air needs an adjustment."

That last part seemed to make sense to Natalie. She thought for a few seconds and then she shook Ashley's hand. "Fine."

If this was a patience test, Ashley was determined to get an A. "So . . . here's how it works, Natalie." They were still shaking hands. "When someone forgives you, then it's your turn."

Natalie removed her hand and crossed her arms. "My turn to what?"

"To apologize." The girl really didn't know much about these things. "Because forgiveness comes *after* an apology." Ashley almost felt sorry for Natalie. "But I overlooked that by going first this time."

Natalie was struggling to say sorry, that much was clear. But after a long moment she surrendered. "Okay." She looked down and mumbled to the floor. "I'm sorry."

"Eyes, please." Ashley pointed to her eyeballs. "Apology has to happen eye to eye."

Again Natalie made a face. "You're very difficult, Ashley Baxter." She looked right into Ashley's eyes. "I'm sorry. There."

Her plan was working! Ashley was making the most of her day and now mean-girl Natalie had actually apologized! "Thank you, Natalie." Ashley patted the girl's shoulder like she was Luke's age. "And I'm actually not difficult."

That was it. The end of their discussion. But this was a start. Maybe one day Natalie would be an unlikely friend, too.

Everything about Monday was going great until lunchtime.

Ashley was walking to the table to sit with Kari, Liza, and Mandy. Plus also Marsha. At the sleepover, the girls had made a plan to ask Marsha to sit with them from now on. So today that was happening.

But halfway to the table a boy named Chris from Landon Blake's table stood and blocked Ashley's way. "Nice hair." His grin wasn't altogether friendly.

*Think the best,* Ashley told herself. *It's up to me.* She put her shoulders back and smiled. "Why, thank you, Chris."

He laughed. "You think I'm serious?" He looked at the other boys at his table and then back at her. His face was meaner than before. "You look like Peter Pan."

With every piece of her heart, Ashley wanted to change this moment. This day was a gift. So why was Chris making fun of her? She tried to step around the rude boy. "Excuse me. I need to get by."

But Chris cut her off again. Ashley felt her knees knock together. She had to get away from this boy. Because tears stung at the corners of her eyes. And she couldn't cry here. No matter what.

Chris made a pose and pointed to the ceiling, like he was pretending to be Peter Pan. "Look who's here!" He stared at her. "Peter herself." This made some of the boys at his table laugh.

Everyone except Landon Blake.

At those mean words from Chris, Landon rushed to his feet. "Hey." He barked the word. "Knock it off!"

Chris stopped laughing. "What?" He seemed like he was trying to sound tough. "Her hair *is* short."

"Listen." Landon took another step toward him. "That's rude." He glanced at Ashley. "Besides, short hair is better for her sport." Landon gave Ashley a secret grin. Then he turned angry eyes back to Chris. "Ashley is a gymnast." He gave Chris a tough nudge on his shoulder. "And she's supergood at it. So leave her alone."

The shirt Chris was wearing was lopsided from Landon's nudging. Chris fixed it and sat down. Real quiet. And in a rude voice, he mumbled under his breath. "I didn't know you two were *friends*."

Ashley didn't know, either. She looked at Landon. He seemed to find his control. He stared straight at Chris. "Well . . . we are. And I like her short hair."

Ashley couldn't believe it. Landon defending her like this. She blinked back her tears and looked at Landon. "Thanks," she whispered.

Landon's smile was the nicest Ashley had ever seen. He shrugged and put his hands in his pockets. He didn't have to say anything.

His actions had done all the talking.

• • •

That afternoon Ashley sat on the couch reading *The Mouse and the Motorcycle*. Ralph the mouse seemed more mischievous with every page. Ashley liked him. And she liked the sketches in the book. For the project she could definitely add some new drawings. Natalie would like that.

Ashley smiled. If not, Natalie would get used to the idea.

She was halfway through the third chapter when Dad asked her to go to the hardware store. Everyone else had plans and he needed a helper. Ashley was up before he finished the question. She loved times when it was just Dad and her.

They bought lightbulbs and batteries for the smoke detectors and putty for the sink. Which was different than Silly Putty, apparently. While they shopped, Ashley told Dad about Elliot, her unlikely friend, and Natalie, and Chris, the mean boy.

And about Landon, who came to her rescue.

"Landon." Dad winked at her. "Wasn't he the menace?"

Ashley giggled. "Not anymore, I guess. He stood up for me."

Dad nodded. "It's important to stand up for others. So bullies don't get their way." He put his hand on her shoulder. "How are you feeling about the move?" Dad's voice got quiet.

"Um . . ." This was not something Ashley wanted to talk about. She looked at her shoes and bit the inside of her cheek. "I didn't have a choice. No one asked me if I wanted to move." She wasn't being disrespectful, but she was impatient. She wiped at a pesky tear trying to make its way down her face. "I just miss home. And my school. And Lydia. I'm not the happiest right now about this particular chapter."

Her dad turned and faced her. "Some chapters are hard. It's okay to miss those things." He pulled her into a hug that lasted a long time. And afterward, Ashley felt a lot better.

He didn't tell her she had to be happy or that she had no choice. He just let her say whatever she was feeling. And sometimes that's what mattered most. Someone to listen and give you a hug.

On the way back to their car, they passed the old art gallery. "Can we look?" Ashley only wanted to see the pieces that hung in the front.

"I was just going to ask if you wanted to walk over here!" Dad took her hand and led her to the window display.

At first Ashley couldn't talk. The paintings were too beautiful for words.

Dad put his arm around her. "Ashley . . . ?"

"I'm memorized." She didn't want to blink. That way she wouldn't miss a single second of their beauty.

Her dad laughed. "*Mesmerized.* That's the word you're looking for."

Ashley squinted. "I like *memorized*. Because I'm looking very intensely so I can memorize this beautiful work." She stared at the paintings again. Who had created these and what was the story behind each one? She looked up at her father. "Amazing, right, Daddy?"

"Yes." He angled his head, his eyes right on hers. "You know what?"

"What?" Ashley waited.

"One day your work is going to be right here. In this display." He hugged her close. "Someone has to be the next professional artist. I think she'll be you!"

Her excitement was so great, Ashley had to close her eyes. Because this was what love felt like.

Having her daddy believe in her.

Back at the house, Ashley helped her dad change lightbulbs, replace batteries, and smear putty on the pipe beneath the kitchen sink. And when they were all finished, Dad pulled something out of a bag.

A brand-new box of coloring pencils!

"I had fun with you today." He kissed her cheek. "Can't wait to see what you draw!" He smiled at her. "Remember, Ashley, the chapters in our lives never last forever. Even the sad ones end and one day you'll turn the page and you'll wake up and you'll be happy. I promise."

"You're the best daddy in the world." Ashley hugged him. "You saved the day."

The rest of the night, Ashley sketched a picture of Natalie and her on a motorcycle. Natalie's arms were crossed, not quite enjoying the ride. But in the drawing Ashley was shouting and laughing, one arm raised. Because this book report could be the thing that made Natalie and Ashley finally be friends. As she sketched, she thought about something else. If she could find a connection with Elliot and even Natalie, then one day she might have one more unlikely friend.

A boy named Landon Blake.

# 16

## Mom's Birthday Disaster

### KARI

Kari's hand was tired, but she stirred the cake batter as fast as she could. Throwing a surprise party took a lot of work. And now they needed to really move because they were running out of time.

She stared into the batter. Her hand wasn't the only thing in a cramp. Her heart was, too. Because every time she wanted to tell her parents the truth about her cheating day, something got in the way. Not once had there been a good time. Or, at least that's how it seemed.

Including today, since this was Mom's birthday!

The surprise party had been Kari's idea, but everyone wanted to help. Brooke was in charge of dinner—baked chicken, sweet potato fries, and salad. Erin, Luke, and Ashley were running around decorating, and Dad was at the store picking up their mom's gift. Luke was feeling much better since his fall, and he had been quite the trouper with his cast.

Kari was in charge of making the cake.

She checked the time. Thirty minutes and Mom would be home. Their mother's friend, Miss Elaine, had taken her shopping. Miss Elaine was in on the surprise. She was providing the perfect distraction so the kids could pull the party together.

Kari dipped her finger in the batter and took a quick taste. "Mmm!"

"No tasting." Brooke grabbed a paper towel and dried her sweaty face. "It's hot in here. We have to hurry."

"Scotch tape, please!" Ashley yelled from the hallway.

Brooke was stirring something on the stove. "In here. On the table."

Ashley ran into the kitchen and grabbed the tape just as Kari took another quick taste.

"I saw that." Ashley grinned. "Is it good?"

"The best!" Kari held her fingers together. "The cook has to taste the batter. Bon appétit!"

"I agree!" Ashley came closer and stared at the cake batter. "Because *bon appétit* means you have a better appetite if the food has no bones!" She looked confident about this. "Like cake."

"No." Brooke glanced at Ashley as she checked the chicken and sweet potatoes. "*Bon appétit* means you hope the meal tastes good."

*Amazing.* Kari looked over her shoulder at Brooke. "How do you know so much?"

"Experience." She closed the oven door. "Because I'm in eighth grade."

"Understandable." Ashley raced back to the front door. "I hope the tape works. The banner won't stay up!"

Brooke turned to Kari. "When's Dad coming back?"

"Any minute." Kari laughed. The craziness was kind of fun. "I can't wait to see the gift."

The kids had chipped in their money to get Mom an orange and black striped cat clock for the living room wall. A few weeks ago Kari had been shopping with Mom when they spotted the clock. Kari thought it was the cutest thing ever. And Mom agreed. "Yes." She had smiled. "It's very cute."

That had settled it. The clock was the perfect birthday gift.

The cake was ready for the oven. Kari opened one cupboard, then another, but the pans were nowhere. "Help!" she yelled. "Anyone know where the cake pan is?"

Ashley ran with the banner and tape back down the hallway. "Next to the fridge!" She sounded frantic. "I need thumbtacks for this thing!"

Kari found the pan, greased it, and filled it with cake batter. "Brooke . . . can I put the cake in the oven? The chicken and sweet potatoes are taking all the space!"

"Hold on, I'm helping Ashley with the banner!" After a minute, Brooke ran back into the kitchen and opened the oven door. "Use the highest rack." She gave Kari a quick look. "Just watch so it doesn't burn."

"Okay." Kari took hold of the full pan and

moved with slow steps to the oven. *Careful,* she told herself. *No time for spills.* Slowly, she slid the pan in and shut the door.

Just then Dad hurried in from the garage. "Cat clock mission accomplished!" He sounded as excited as the kids. He took a deep sniff. "Smells wonderful." He gave Kari a fast hug and walked toward the entryway. She could hear his happy voice. "This looks perfect! She'll be so surprised!"

Kari followed her dad and looked around. He was right. The streamers cascaded down the staircase and the banner was tacked up in the perfect spot so Mom could see it when she walked through the front door. Kari turned to their dad. "Let's see the clock. I've been waiting forever for this!"

Dad pulled a box out of the shopping bag. "I can't believe the tail moves with every second." Dad grinned at the kids, and then handed the box to Luke, who balanced it on his cast. "Let's get it wrapped."

"Good idea." Kari nodded to Luke and Erin. "You two can wrap it. Mom will love that."

Back in the kitchen, Dad met with Kari and

Brooke and Ashley. He peered into the oven. "Wow." He smiled. "I'm impressed."

"It was all Kari's idea." Ashley beamed at Kari across the kitchen. "Which I must admit is the most thoughtful thing you've done all year."

Kari laughed. "Thanks." She made a silly face. "I think."

Brooke placed the potholders on the counter near the oven. "Mom deserves a surprise party!"

A clean kitchen would be another surprise, so Kari quick washed the cake bowl and spatula. She was drying it when she heard Erin laughing in the living room. She was about to tell her little sister to be serious. They had to wrap the clock before—

*Crack!*

The terrible sound echoed through the house. At the same time, Erin screamed.

In a flash, Kari and her sisters and Dad raced into the living room. Kari was first on the scene. "What happened?" Kari stared at the situation. "Erin?"

The youngest Baxter girl was standing smack in the middle of the cat box. "Sorry." She tiptoed out of the mess. "I was dancing with Luke and . . . I tripped."

"No." Kari's word was more of a cry. Not the cat clock. She dropped to the floor and pulled the damaged box close. Brooke helped her open it, and then with much caution, Kari pulled the clock out. "Oh, no!"

The tail was missing.

Kari dug around in the box and pulled it out—in three pieces. "I can't believe this."

Dad put his hand on the top of her head. "Erin's sorry." He peered at the broken cat. "I think we can fix it."

Luke shook his head. "I don't think so."

"All our allowance money." Ashley shook her head. "Smashed by a single foot."

Erin covered her face and ran to the sofa. "I'm so sorry." She curled up in a ball.

"Kids." Their dad gave them a warning look. "Erin didn't mean to break the cat clock." He walked over and sat on the sofa beside her, and he put his hand on her back. "Let's not hurt her feelings."

He had a point. Kari felt bad. She shouldn't care more about the cat's tail than Erin's feelings. She joined Dad at the sofa, and Brooke and Ashley and Luke did the same thing. They all patted Erin's head and shoulders.

Finally Erin sat up and looked around. Her eyes were red. "I ruined everything."

"No." Luke grinned. "Mom will still like it." He looked back at the broken pieces on the floor. "Now it's one of a kind."

"And we still have the decorations and the dinner," Dad said. "Brooke made the best—"

*Beep . . . Beep . . . Beep!*

A shrill siren cut through the house. Dad was on his feet racing for the kitchen. "Something's burning!"

*"My chicken!"* Brooke screamed as she ran off.

"Save the fries!" Luke yelled back.

Kari and the others followed, and when they rounded the corner into the kitchen they all froze. Smoke billowed out the oven door like from a chimney. Brooke waved her hand in front of her face and coughed. "Quick! Someone open a window!"

"Open the door!" Dad yelled above the noise of the alarm. He motioned to Ashley. "And all the windows!"

Smoke filled the whole kitchen and the alarm was still screeching through the house.

"I'm outta here." Luke grabbed the tape and ran back toward the living room.

Kari couldn't believe it. How had everything gone so wrong? The surprise birthday party was ruined. "Should we call the fire department?"

"There's no fire." Brooke was waving off the smoke with a dish towel. "It was the sweet potato fries."

Everyone had to shout to be heard above the blaring siren.

"Honey, let me." Dad took over. He pulled out a tray and set it on the counter. Black crispy pieces of ash sat where the sweet potato slices used to be. For a few seconds he just stared at the smoky mess. "Well." He looked at Kari. "We still have the chicken."

Dad grabbed the chicken dish and set it on the

counter. Kari stared at it and shook her head. "It looks . . ."

"Like chicken jerky." Ashley waved her hand in front of her nose. "It smells terrible."

*Beep . . . Beep . . . Beep.*

Suddenly Kari gasped. "My cake!" The siren was so loud it hurt Kari's ears. She wanted to rescue her cake, but her dad was on it. He pulled it from the oven and Kari felt her heart sink. "Noooo."

The cake was fully black. Like it had been frosted in ashes.

Ashley squinted through the smoke. "Maybe if we cut off a layer from the top and sides?" She placed her hands over her ears. "Good thing we changed the batteries, huh, Daddy?"

"Yes, Ashley!" He laughed. "Good thing!" The smoke was clearing a little. Dad climbed up on a chair and held the button in the center of the smoke detector.

At that very minute, Mom came into the kitchen from the front door. Kari and her siblings turned and stared at her. Not a single person spoke. The alarm was still screaming through the house.

*Beep . . . Beep—*

Just then Dad got the noise to stop. And everything went silent.

Mom covered her mouth, apparently speechless.

"Surprise!" Kari broke the deafening postalarm silence. She held up her hands and let them fall to her sides. "Happy Birthday!"

Mom's smile took up her whole face. "I can't believe this!" She coughed a few times. "You kids are amazing!" She held out her arms, and Kari and the others ran to her. The group hug lasted a long while.

"Yes." Dad coughed and shook his head. "It's been quite the exciting afternoon."

Ashley stepped back. "Did you see our decorations? They didn't catch fire!" She took their Mom's hand. "Come on!"

Kari and the others followed. When they reached the foyer, Mom gasped as she looked around. Kari managed a weak smile. The decorations were still pretty wonderful.

Their mom was circling the foyer. "This is

incredible! I didn't really look before." She grinned at each of them. "I sort of ran through . . . because I thought the house was on fire."

"Yes." Ashley nodded. "That would be a distraction. Definitely."

"This is just . . ." Mom's eyes looked damp. Like she might cry. "It's so thoughtful of you kids."

Ashley pointed at Kari. "It was her idea." She linked arms with Kari and then Brooke and Erin. "But we all pitched in."

"You kids mean the world to me. I feel so special." She looked at Dad. "Where's Luke?"

"Here!" He came running into the entryway. In his hands was a strange-shaped wrapped gift.

Kari put her hand to her face. Luke hadn't used the box. Probably because it was crushed. She lowered her hand and grinned at him. Her brother had at least tried. "Thanks, Luke."

Luke held the gift out to their mom. "This is for you." He had tape stuck to his cheek and arm, but he had never looked more joyful. "Happy Birthday!"

"What's this?" Their mom took the package.

She led the group back to the living room, where she sat in the nearest chair. "I had no idea."

This was the moment Kari had waited for. Maybe Luke had found a way to fix it. She held her breath while Mom unwrapped the gift.

All of a sudden their mother's eyes got very big. "Okay. Wow." She looked speechless. "A . . . cat clock."

Kari bounced a little, until she actually saw the gift. It was covered in Scotch tape. She felt her enthusiasm disappear like the smoke in the kitchen. "It's . . . the one you said was cute." Her smile felt like it was struggling. "Remember?"

"Yes." Mom gave a few slow nods. "I certainly do." She lifted it, and as she did, the tail fell off.

"It's broken." Luke shrugged. "I tried to fix it."

"I can maybe make it work again." Ashley put her arm on their mother's shoulder. "You know, Mom. I'm a pretty good handy girl. I can fix anything." Ashley sent a grin to their father. "Right, Daddy?"

Dad winked at her. "Right!"

Mom giggled. "Well, then, perfect!" She pulled

Kari close. "I love it, sweetheart. So considerate of you." She looked at the others. "All of you."

"The dinner, on the other hand"—Brooke took their mom's hand—"cannot be fixed."

"I figured." Mom was still laughing. "It doesn't matter. This is the best birthday surprise."

Dad decided they would all go to Tradewinds in downtown Bloomington, Mom's favorite restaurant. Mom ordered chicken—in honor of Brooke's choice for dinner.

Kari thought that was a nice touch.

While they ate, Mom told them about a special birthday memory. "When I turned ten I got my first pair of roller skates. I still remember the wind in my face as I raced around the neighborhood that day." For a minute, yesterday shone in her eyes. Then she smiled big. "But this birthday is my *favorite*. I love you all so much." She looked around the table, happy tears in her eyes.

"We love you, too." Kari slid closer to her mother. "You're the best mom we ever had."

"And the only one." Mom's tone was sweet and

her smile became a quiet laugh. "Thank you." She kissed Kari's head. "You're the best *kids* I've ever had."

After dinner, Dad had an idea. "Let's go across the street for ice cream!"

"Yes!" The others were on their feet, walking with Dad.

All at once Kari saw her opportunity. "Dad!" she called after him. "I . . . need to talk to Mom. We'll be there in a few minutes."

Dad looked back at her. "Okay!" He waved. "Don't take too long."

When he was gone, Kari turned to her mom. "I'm glad you liked the decorations. So at least there was one good thing about today." With every word, Kari became more certain. This was finally the time to tell her mother the truth.

"What do you mean?" Mom looked confused. "The whole day has been perfect."

"Not the whole day. Not this part." Kari sighed. "I have to tell you something." Her heart began to pound. "I . . . wanted to wait for a day that wasn't your birthday. But . . ." Tears filled her eyes. "I can't take it anymore."

"It's okay, honey." Her mother patted her back. "Slow down. What happened?"

Kari took a deep breath. How could she have waited so long to say this? She could feel the words building and suddenly the story began to pour out. "So . . . a few weeks ago we had a history quiz. Only I never read the chapters."

"You didn't?" Mom sounded concerned.

"No." Kari felt sick to her stomach. This talk was harder than she had thought. "So . . ." She squeezed her eyes shut. "I cheated. I stole the answers, Mom." Kari's eyes blinked open. "I looked at the boy's paper next to me. So I would get an A."

Mom's eyes were wide. Like she couldn't believe this sad story.

Kari hung her head. "I deserve to be punished. Or kicked out of school." Her voice faded. "Possibly kicked out of the family."

Her mom was quiet for a moment and then she cleared her throat. "So . . . you cheated to get a good grade?"

"Yes." Kari raised her eyebrows. "It isn't my style to get a bad grade."

This time her mother was silent for a long moment. "Cheating always ends poorly." She sounded kind. Stern but kind. "Telling the truth on the other hand . . . always ends well."

Kari sniffed. "I've wanted to tell you for so long."

Mom took Kari's hand. "I'm so glad you told me. You can always tell me anything. Your surprise party was an amazing gift, but you telling the truth about cheating . . . that's the best gift of all."

Kari held her breath. "So . . . I won't get kicked out of the family?"

Her mom looked at her, straight to her heart. "How did it feel to carry your cheating around . . . all this time?"

"Terrible." A tear slid down Kari's cheek. "Like I was carrying rocks on my back."

"Remember that." Mom kissed her cheek. "Telling the truth always makes you feel better."

Kari felt herself relax, and freedom came over her. The best feeling of freedom ever. "I'll remember."

"Still . . ." Her mom hesitated. "You need to tell your father . . . and someone else."

"Who?" Kari thought about her siblings. They would be so disappointed in her.

Mom sounded very serious. "You need to tell your teacher."

Kari frowned. She couldn't imagine telling her teacher. But her mother was right. She nodded. "Okay. I'll tell Daddy tonight. And Ms. Nan as soon as possible."

"That's my good girl. And remember, you don't have to get an A every time. Part of learning is working through a bad grade."

"Yes." Kari nodded. "I know that now."

Mom took Kari's hand and the two of them walked across the street to the ice cream shop. Kari felt so much better. They had given their mother a nice gift with the surprise party.

But even better was the gift of telling the truth. And now, for the first time since she'd cheated, Kari felt light on her feet. Which made sense.

The rocks were gone.

# 17

# Lost at the Zoo

### ASHLEY

The sea animal reports turned out to be the best fun in all of fifth grade.

Ashley acted out the movements of an octopus in front of the other students and at the end of her performance the entire class clapped. Also some of them laughed, but Ashley felt like they were laughing with her.

Which gave her another chance to curtsy. Mr. Garrett gave her an A, and Ashley decided hers was the best report in the class.

Except Landon's was maybe a close second place. Because Landon made a life-size sea turtle out of paper and glue.

Then, after the reports, Mr. Garrett had surprised them with an announcement. They were going to the zoo for a special field trip!

And now the day for the zoo was here!

Ashley rushed to the front of the line for boarding the bus, which meant she'd have to sit at the back. She didn't care.

A zoo field trip was the highlight of all her days in Bloomington! Back home, her family went to the zoo every year. But they'd never been to the Indianapolis Zoo.

Ashley settled into her seat at the back and watched the other kids file onto the bus. Lunch was special today, too. Her mom had packed a lion-shaped peanut butter sandwich, gummy bears and animal crackers. For the zoo theme. Also in her backpack was her sketchbook and her favorite new pencils from Dad.

Because sketching animals at the zoo was an artist's dream.

Finally everyone was on board, but they couldn't leave. Chris and his friends up front were making loud sounds and laughing like hyenas. Ashley rolled her eyes. "Who won't grow up now?" she whispered to herself.

Mr. Garrett stood at the front near the driver. "Would you boys like to spend the day in the office?"

Ashley giggled quietly. Apparently the answer was no, because the boys quieted down right away. *Gotta love that Mr. Garrett,* she thought to herself. A late girl hurried onto the bus and down the aisle. There was an open seat by Ashley, so the girl sat down.

"Hi." Ashley scooted closer to the window so the girl had room. "I'm Ashley. You sit in the back of the class, right?"

The girl laughed. "I do. I'm Amy." She had friendly brown eyes. "You sit up front, right?"

"Yep." Ashley smiled. This was nice. Why hadn't she met Amy earlier? She was so much nicer than Natalie. Amy was friendly and good at conversations. Easier to talk to than quiet Natalie. Ashley smiled at Amy. "You sit next to those boys, I think."

"Yes. Right next to Chris Parker." Amy rolled her eyes. "It's been a very loud year so far." She laughed.

"Oh, I believe you." Ashley relaxed in her seat. "So what's your favorite animal? Mine's the giraffe. Those huge brown spots and their long necks."

Amy shifted, maybe so she could see Ashley better. "Mine's the elephant! I like their trunks!" Amy raised her arm in the air and trumpeted like an elephant. When she did, her two pretty blond braids swayed like elephant ears.

They both laughed. Amy was actually a *likely* friend. A friend from the first minute. Ashley looked a few rows ahead and she spotted not-so-likely Natalie, sitting alone. Talking to no one. Ashley almost felt sorry for her.

Amy was still talking about elephants and how the babies were even cuter than the grown-ups.

Ashley nodded. "They are so cute!" Then she glanced ahead at Natalie again. *Hmm,* she thought. Maybe with a little more effort things could be different. Maybe Natalie wasn't *trying* to be mean. Sure, she kept to herself. And, well, she was usually grouchy. But there could be a reason. Because everyone was different. And everyone deserved a chance.

That's what Ashley's dad always said.

Amy had turned around to talk to the girls behind them. Ashley leaned in close. "I'm gonna sit next to my book report partner." She raised her eyebrows. "So much work ahead."

"Okay." Amy smiled. "Nice meeting you."

"You, too." Ashley slid out of the seat and walked up to Natalie. She was reading their class book. Ashley made a small cough sound. "Excuse me." She made her eyes a little wider. "Hello."

Natalie jumped like she'd been stung by a bee. Then she settled down and frowned. "What?"

Not exactly a warm welcome. Ashley pressed on. "Mind if I sit here?"

Natalie slid over to make some room.

"Okay." Ashley would need double patience for this girl. "I'll take that as a yes." She dropped to the open seat, and tried to think of something to say. "So . . ." Ashley found her most upbeat voice. "Are you having a good week?"

"No." Natalie crossed her arms and looked out the window.

"Hmm." How was she supposed to figure Natalie out? What would it take to make her laugh? Ashley tapped Natalie's shoulder. "Have you been to the zoo before?"

Natalie looked back at her. "No."

"What?" Ashley practically stood up. "Never?" She couldn't imagine such a thing. Ashley tapped her chin. "Have you been on a field trip?"

"No." Natalie turned and faced Ashley. She sighed.

That was all Ashley could take. She stood and stared at the girl. "Do you ever say *anything* but *no*?"

For the first time, Natalie didn't have that stuck-up expression. She pressed herself back against the window, and looked very shocked.

Ashley dropped to her seat. "I had to get that off my chest." She waited. "Still hoping for an answer over here."

Natalie looked out the window again for a minute, and then back at Ashley. She hesitated. "I just . . . sometimes I don't want to talk."

Ashley's patience officially ran out. Nothing worked with Natalie. Nothing! Ashley leaned forward and rested her head on the seat back in front of her. But after a moment she felt a tap on her shoulder. She lifted her head, looked at Natalie, and whispered, "Can I help you?"

"Yes." Natalie's voice was quiet, too. "Thanks for sitting by me." Natalie didn't seem to want anyone to hear her.

For a few seconds, Ashley watched Natalie. The slightest smile lifted the corners of the girl's mouth. Ashley took a deep breath. Somewhere deep inside Natalie there had to be an actual big smile. Maybe even a laugh. Ashley forced herself to believe it.

But at least Natalie had given her a tiny smile. It wasn't a lot. But, it would have to do.

A buzz went through the bus and Ashley looked out the window. The zoo! They were here! Ashley's feet had trouble staying still. She wanted off this thing.

Before they could leave, Mr. Garrett stood at the front of the bus and explained the rules. "Everyone stay with a buddy. No running. Don't get left behind." He pumped his fist in the air. "And . . . have fun!"

The students cheered and clapped and grabbed their backpacks with their sack lunches. And soon they were on their way, walking through the zoo.

At the first stop, three black bears lumbered around a patch of grass and big rocks. Next came the funny pink flamingos, and then the sleepy rhinos.

Ashley could barely breathe the whole time. Animals were perfection. She couldn't take her eyes off them. They were so beautiful! God must have had fun coming up with the bear's furry skin and the flamingo's skinny legs and the rhino's fierce horn. Did God sketch the animals before He made them?

Ashley skipped along. Probably, He did. Because He was the best artist.

Just then they reached the giraffes!

Mr. Garrett read the sign out loud. "Giraffes are the tallest mammals on Earth." He looked around the class. "Elliot, what's a mammal?"

Elliot paused, thinking about his answer.

"They're warm-blooded. They feed their young with milk." He paused until the answer hit him. "And they have hair!"

"Good." Mr. Garrett told them that the giraffes' legs were about six feet tall. Just the legs. He started talking about what they ate and how they ate.

Ashley looked around and spotted a bench just behind her class. It wasn't far from where Landon Blake stood, listening to their teacher. She moved in a hurry past Landon. This was her chance. She sat down and quick as she could, she pulled her sketchbook and three pencils from her backpack.

Then she studied the giraffes. She had to draw one of those guys. Otherwise the trip would be a fail.

Starting at the bottom of the animal, Ashley drew the giraffe with the most careful care. She sketched four long skinny legs, then the body and finally the long neck and pretty face. With every stroke of her pencil, she glanced up at the majestic animal. Then back to her paper, then back to the giraffe. She had to get every detail just right.

Because when would she have this chance again?

She was busy filling in the tree branches and leaves, which the giraffe was eating, when Mr. Garrett announced they were leaving.

"Stay together." He looked back straight at her. "Come on, Ashley!"

Clearly, her teacher was not waiting around. "Almost done." Ashley said the words out loud, but not quite loud enough for her teacher to hear. She saw the class walk around the corner, disappearing from sight.

*Hurry,* she told herself. *You have to hurry.* She had saved the best part for last. "The spots have to be perfect." Her voice was very quiet. All her attention was on the giraffe.

That's when she noticed Landon Blake. He was still standing there, watching her. "They're going." He sounded concerned. "We should go, too. So we don't get lost."

Ashley kept drawing. "No one's making you stay." Why did Landon care whether she got lost or not?

"I'm not leaving you alone." Frustration filled between his words. "Buddy system . . ."

She rolled her eyes and kept drawing. "I'm fine, Landon." Ashley finished the spots and shaded in the giraffe's shadow. Finally she closed her book. "See. I'm done!" She gave Landon a smirk. "Nothing to worry about." She scanned the area around her. "Where'd they go?"

Landon shrugged. "I don't know. I was watching you."

"Why?" Ashley was annoyed. "If you'd paid more attention, we wouldn't be lost."

"I was staring at your drawing." Landon's smile started in his eyes. "It's really good."

Ashley sighed. "Thanks. But now we need to find the others." She took off, scanning the path for Mr. Garrett. Landon followed her. They looked in every possible direction.

No sign of the class.

"Come on . . . this way." Landon took the lead and they ran to the Reptile Encounter. It was pitch dark inside.

"Mr. Garrett?" Ashley tried to whisper. But it came out kind of loud like a hiss.

Landon laughed. "You sound like a snake." He hissed back at her.

Ashley furrowed her brow. "I do not." She kept walking. Her eyes were getting used to the dark room. Snakes slithered around in lighted aquariums on both sides.

"Don't get bit!" Landon poked Ashley's side.

She screamed and jumped ahead. "Hey!" She giggled. "Quit!"

"Shhh!" One of the zoo workers turned toward Landon and Ashley. "Where's your teacher?" The zoo worker started to come their way. His face looked reddish and his eyebrows sat low on his face.

"Let's get out of here!" Ashley's voice was louder than before.

"We should ask him for help!" Landon hesitated.

But Ashley was already running for the exit. She called out over her shoulder. "He'll put us in the zoo jail!"

Ashley wasn't sure if there was a zoo jail. But it sounded possible. And she definitely didn't want to go there. She kept running.

Landon caught up to her. "You're right. We can find our class by ourselves."

"Exactly." Ashley was glad Landon understood. "It would be terrible to spend the rest of the year in zoo jail."

"Hey! You kids, stop!" The zoo worker called after them.

"Come on!" Landon took Ashley's hand. "Run!"

They ran through the encounter, out the other side, past the monkeys, the meerkats and the crocodiles. Landon kept looking back and he only stopped after he seemed sure they weren't being followed. They were near the elephants, and totally exhausted. Ashley let go of Landon's hand and put her hands on her head. Landon crossed his arms.

They were both breathing fast.

After a few seconds Ashley looked at the sea of people behind them. "I think we avoided zoo jail."

Landon crossed his arms. "So what do we do now, Miss nothing-to-worry-about?" He was only teasing. Ashley could tell, now.

"I have no answers." She leaned on a fence post. "We are officially lost. And it was all my fault." She hated that Landon was right. But he was. Ashley's heart beat a bit faster. "What if we never find them?" Panic raced through her.

"I guess we just stay here forever." He pretended to look scared. "Maybe work here." Landon broke into a laugh. "We'll probably have to clean up after the elephants."

"Not funny." Ashley searched the crowd again. Where were they? Surely Mr. Garrett didn't take the kids back to school without them. But there was no sign of their class.

"We might as well keep walking." Landon led them to the lions. "We're a couple of wilderness explorers, Ashley. You and me." He grinned. "Which is actually pretty fun."

"Yeah." Ashley smiled. This definitely was turning out to be better than she expected. "We're good explorers."

"We are." Landon stopped at the big cats. "I like lions the best."

Ashley studied the animals. Their huge paws and wild manes. "They're my scariest." She looked a little longer. One lion yawned and shook his hairy head. His tail swished this way and that. His eyes looked fierce. That's when Ashley started to see it. "I guess they are beautiful."

"Exactly. And strong!" Landon nodded. "We should get closer."

The lions were pacing. Like they were hungry. Ashley followed Landon to the spot right by the enclosure.

After a bit, Ashley didn't look at the lions. She

looked at Landon. "Hey." Her voice was softer. "I never got to thank you for what you did after I got my haircut."

He looked confused. "What do you mean?"

"You know. With Chris and the whole Peter Pan thing." Ashley shrugged. She felt a little shy. "It was just really nice."

"Oh . . . that. No big deal." Landon seemed to brush it off. "Chris jokes too much. Someone had to stop him."

Ashley laughed. "It was a big deal to me." All people who were ever bullied should have someone like Landon to defend them.

Just then Ashley spotted a familiar face. "Look!" There in the crowd was Mr. Garrett. He was walking with a security guard. Ashley motioned to Landon to follow her. "It's our class. Let's go."

She took off toward their teacher, and Landon followed.

As soon as she got close enough she ran right into her teacher's arms. "You're here!" She was out of breath again. "I thought we were going to be stuck in this place forever."

Mr. Garrett stepped back and stared at Ashley. "Where have you been?" He let out a long breath. Like he was extra tired from looking. "We've searched everywhere for you two." His eyes moved to Landon. "We were very worried."

"I'm sorry." If Ashley told the truth, she could get in trouble. But she also didn't want to lie. She sucked in through her teeth. "I was sketching and—"

"It was all my fault," Landon cut her off. He looked at Ashley. "I was talking to her . . . about her sketches. We got distracted."

What was he doing? Ashley gave Landon a look of amazement. He didn't have to defend her. That was something only friends do. Plus, the security guard looked ready to handcuff someone. Maybe Landon really would be shipped off to zoo jail.

All for her.

Then she remembered her thought from the other day when he'd helped her with Chris. Maybe Landon Blake was actually becoming an unlikely friend.

"Hmm." Mr. Garrett gave Landon a stern look.

But it didn't last long. "I guess I'm just glad you're both safe." He thanked the security guard and sent him on his way.

Relief washed over Ashley as she watched the man go. No handcuffs. Not today. Her next breath felt more relaxed. "Where's everyone else?" She tried to smile, but it didn't seem like a very good idea. Not when she and Landon Blake were basically fugitives.

Mr. Garrett raised his brow. "They're waiting on the bus. It's time to go." Their teacher stopped for a minute and shook his head. "Ashley . . . why is it that you're always on the other end of these things?"

"I don't know." She held her hands out to the sides. "Talent?" A recent memory hit her. "Also, Mr. Garrett, I did get a very nice sketch of a giraffe out of the whole ordeal. I thought I should mention that." She shrugged. "So that actually is talent."

A laugh came from Mr. Garrett even as he tried to stop it. "Yes, Ashley. You're very talented."

As they followed their teacher back to the bus, Landon stayed by Ashley's side. Halfway there she glanced at him and mouthed, "Thank you."

He nodded, and a smile moved up to his eyes.

Ashley got onto the bus right after Landon. He took the only completely open seat, close to the front. For a second, Ashley thought about sitting beside him. After all, they were co-explorers. Co-fugitives. She looked at him and he looked at her. Then they grinned at each other one last time.

He was a kind boy, that Landon Blake. But instead of sitting next to him, she walked to the back. Natalie was there, all alone.

"Hi." Ashley took the seat next to that girl. "So . . . wow! What a zoo day, huh?"

"I can't believe you got lost." Natalie's eyes grew wide.

"I can." Ashley made a nervous face. "I was sketching. It was bound to happen."

The girls ate their lunches and talked the whole bus ride back. Between Elliot and then Landon, and now Natalie, this had turned into quite a friendship day. Which could only mean Mr. Garrett was right. An unlikely friend was the best kind of all. She smiled to herself.

Especially when he kept you out of zoo jail.

# 18

## Purple and Gold Memories

### KARI

When their dad told them they were going to Bloomington High School that Friday night for the big football game, Kari had no idea what to expect. The family had never been to a real live high school football game.

But as they walked through the stadium gates and found their seats in the bleachers with the Howards, the excitement and music and stadium lights were more than Kari could've imagined. No wonder Mom and Dad couldn't wait to bring them here!

Even better was the happy light way Kari felt. Both her parents knew about her cheating now. So the only thing left to do was tell her teacher. So far there hadn't been a good time.

Across the field in the bleachers was the school's marching band. The music was loud and bouncy and amazing. "Don't you love it?" Kari raised her voice in Ashley's direction.

"Love it?" Ashley stood and marched in place for a few beats. "I'm joining the band as soon as I set foot in high school." She pointed at the drummers. "I'll have that tall hat and those gold buttons. I'll be the best drummer out there."

"Yes." Kari could picture it. She laughed. "I'm sure you will!"

They settled into their seats, and Kari looked around. Everyone was decked out in Bloomington High purple and gold. They wore T-shirts and sweatshirts and baseball caps, and everything said "BHS" or "Home of the Eagles." The high school girls wore purple and gold ribbons in their hair and pom-poms on their shoes.

The game hadn't started yet but on the field someone was running around in an eagle costume. He threw candy into the high school student section.

"This is amazing." Kari leaned close to her mother. "Let's come every Friday night!"

Mom grinned. "That would make your father happy."

The Howards were extra-festive for the game. Marsha and Carly and their mother had purple and gold glitter on their cheeks and Mr. Howard wore a jersey with Steven's number.

Steven was a running back. Whatever that meant.

"Here." Mrs. Howard handed two tubes of glitter paint to Kari. "You and your sisters can use this. Just put a swipe under your eyes."

All four Baxter girls and their mom decorated their faces with purple and gold paint, and Dad brought a BHS baseball cap for Luke. Next came the National Anthem. Kari loved this part. They played it before every swim meet, too.

The players from both teams lined up on the field, their hands over their hearts. Kari and her family and the Howards did the same thing.

Not till the song was over did Kari notice the Bloomington High cheerleaders. "There!" She pointed. "That's what I want to do! Cheer for my school!"

Ashley gave her a strange look. "Band would be way more fun." She looked at the field and back at Kari. "All cheerleaders do is bounce around." She shrugged. "I guess. If that's what you want to do."

Kari wanted nothing more. The cute skirts and sweaters. All the girls doing the same cheer. It was like dance and sports all at once.

The game started with a giant kick of the ball. Kari didn't understand how it worked, but midway through the second quarter, Carly and Marsha took Kari and Ashley down near the concession stand. "This is where us younger kids hang out," Carly explained.

Right away Kari spotted someone selling popcorn. Someone she wasn't expecting to see.

Her teacher, Ms. Nan.

Kari gulped. This was her chance.

She looked at her sister. Ashley was talking to boys from her class. Something about a race. Ashley could handle herself for a few minutes at least . . . Kari grabbed a deep breath and stood in Ms. Nan's line. There were two other teachers working behind the counter.

"Next please?" Ms. Nan's voice was loud over the sound of the band.

Kari stepped up to the counter and stood on her tiptoes. "Hello, Ms. Nan."

"Kari!" Ms. Nan smiled big and made her way around the counter. She gave Kari a hug. "Happy Friday!"

"Yes. Well, sort of." Kari paused. "I have to get something off my chest."

Ms. Nan checked the line. "Okay. I can take a quick break." She moved with Kari to a quieter spot a few feet away. "What is it?"

Kari crossed her arms. There was no going back. Once she said what she needed to say, anything could happen. She could be kicked out of school or put on display and shamed before the class. But at this point, she didn't care. She needed to tell the truth. If only the words would come.

"Kari?" Ms. Nan prodded.

"Okay." The words were breaking free, lining up on the other side of Kari's teeth. "Remember the history quiz you gave? On chapters one and two?" *Here we go.* Kari stood strong. "Well . . . I cheated on that quiz, Ms. Nan. I hadn't read the book so I took the answers from the boy next to me."

"Connor." Ms. Nan nodded.

"Yes, it was Connor. And I looked . . ." Kari stopped. "Wait. How did you know?"

Ms. Nan chuckled. "Kari. I've been teaching for a while. You've gotten A's on every assignment. Except that one." She raised her eyebrows and put her hands on her hips. "I was waiting for you to tell me."

Kari's mind was spinning. "So . . . I didn't get an A?" She wondered if she might fall over.

"No, you didn't. That's how I knew you copied Connor. He's been struggling in history. So when your answers matched his almost exactly, and I saw the eraser marks, I knew you had copied him."

"And you were waiting . . . for me to tell you?" Kari couldn't believe it.

"Yes." Ms. Nan's voice was full of understanding. "I wanted it to be your lesson. One even more important than anything you'll learn in history. The lesson of being honest."

Kari steadied herself. She remembered so many days with rocks on her back. "All this time? I'm in shock here."

Her teacher stooped down. "I'm proud of you, Kari. Telling the truth is a life skill. It's part of having good character. And on that one—tonight you get an A plus." Ms. Nan gave Kari another quick hug. "And it's okay to not have all the answers. In history . . . and in life."

Yes. Kari liked that. God had given her two wonderful parents and a kind teacher. Adults who could help when she didn't know the answers. She smiled and peace surrounded her. "Thank you, Ms. Nan." She smiled. "See you Monday."

Ms. Nan waved back. "See you then!" She clapped her hands. "Go, Eagles!"

Kari walked back to Ashley and their friends and a thought occurred to her. Ms. Nan hadn't yelled. She hadn't talked about a punishment or a public confession in front of the class. None of that. Because Ms. Nan had grace.

And that was something Kari would remember forever.

. . .

The next morning was Ashley's big gymnastics meet. Kari couldn't stop smiling, because the whole family was there—the way they were for the swim meet. And sure enough, Ashley got a silver medal for her cartwheel.

Of all things.

Back home, everyone helped Mom decorate for fall. Wreaths of orange and yellow and strings of silky autumn leaves were placed around the kitchen and living room and even on the front porch. Where their pumpkins would sit in a few weeks. The leaves were called garland, and they weren't real. But they looked just like the ones on the ground outside.

Mom was making shepherd's pie and baked apples while homemade cider simmered on the stove. Kari breathed in deep. The house smelled sweet and warm and cozy. She smiled. It smelled like home.

They had an hour before dinner, so after decorating, Luke had an idea. "Let's go for a walk." He raised his brow a few times and looked at Kari

274

and his other sisters. Like he was giving them some kind of secret message. He pointed to the backyard.

Kari knew immediately what he meant. "Great idea." She looked at Brooke. "Should we go out back for . . . a *walk*?"

Brooke caught on. "Definitely!" She stood and slid her shoes on. "Let's go."

Mom was adjusting the string of leaves over the kitchen window. "Have fun!" She smiled at them. "Don't forget dinner."

"Okay!" Kari called back as the group headed outside.

Kari and the other Baxter children ran and jogged and marched through the tree line, to the family rock. The place they were all clearly thinking about. Kari remembered the last time they were here. It was that first full day they lived here. So much had changed since then.

All for the better.

They helped each other up onto the rock and there they took in the beauty around them.

"The leaves are changing." Ashley glanced up

at the trees. "God makes them the most beautiful right before they die."

"Mmm." Brooke angled her head. "I like that." She seemed to think for a minute. Then she looked at each of them. "So . . . how are you all doing?" She hesitated. "I—for one—feel settled."

"Me, too." Erin sat on the smooth surface. "I like Bloomington."

Luke nodded. "We have the best yard. So much to explore." He held his arm up. "My cast comes off in a week. So I guess I learned to be careful on trees." His arm was almost better. Just one more week, and the doctor would take the cast off.

"Or stick to looking for lizards. On the ground." Kari patted Luke's good arm. "And I'm glad you're okay." She leaned back on her hands. " As for me, I'm happy. I like my new friends and swimming." She paused. "And I learned the importance of telling the truth. And not cheating." She had already told the others about the scandal. All of them took the news well. Kari grinned at her siblings. "I think I really love it here."

"Same." Brooke took her time. "Carly is an

amazing friend. I love my classes. And playing in the orchestra. Bloomington is the best." She looked at the faces around her. "And, tonight with us getting ready for fall and Mom's cooking, this really feels like home!"

"Yes!" Luke shouted. "Home sweet home."

"I like that! Home sweet home!" Erin's face lit up. "Plus, Mom's making my favorite cider!"

Ashley was quiet. Kari understood. After all, Ashley had told her about the boy who called her Peter Pan names. And her terrible mud day and the gum hair disaster. And getting lost at the zoo. If anyone wasn't perfectly happy, it would be Ashley.

Kari took her sister's hand. "What about you, Ash?"

Ashley looked at her feet. "I guess . . . I like it better than before." She smiled at Kari and then at the others. "The house is nice." She thought for a second. "I'm starting to make some . . . unlikely friends." She paused. "But for me, home will always be in Michigan. And that's okay."

Kari was satisfied with Ashley's answer. People

have to adjust in their own time. Ashley just needed more days.

"It is okay, Ashley." Brooke sat on the other side of their sister. She put her arm around Ashley. "One day this will feel like home. No rush."

"Right." Erin nodded. "I took my time, and it worked out for me."

On the way back, Kari linked arms with Ashley. "I'm happy about your answer."

They slowed their pace and Ashley leaned her head on Kari's shoulder. "Thanks. A little while ago I was ready to run away. If you remember." Ashley straightened again and smiled. "But I'm pushing through. Even after all the tough chapters."

"I'm glad you didn't leave." Kari nudged her sister. "And look . . . you're choosing joy! It's already getting better. You have Marsha and Natalie and Landon."

Ashley raised one eyebrow. "Don't forgot Elliot. The gum boy." She giggled. "We're an unlikely bunch."

"But they're your friends." Kari put her arm around Ashley's shoulders. "See? God can do anything when we have the right attitude."

"An attitude of gratitude." Ashley smiled. She looked at the house in the distance, and then to Kari. "Race you back!"

Kari pulled away from her sister and headed fast toward home. But as always, Ashley was quicker. She took the lead and reached the back porch first. Inside, Mom was setting the shepherd's pie on the counter. The top was golden brown and bubbly. Next she put the apples on a cooking tray and slid it into the oven.

The perfect fall dinner.

When they were all seated, just before their dad prayed, Kari looked around the table. It was the best autumn night. Mom asked questions about school and what they wanted to do at the Fall Festival. As they talked, Kari looked at Ashley. At one point, maybe even soon, Michigan would be a beautiful memory. Part of the past. Kari believed that. And then Ashley would see Bloomington not only as a place where they lived.

But as the most wonderful home ever.

# 19

## A Fall Festival to Remember

**ASHLEY**

When the bell rang Friday before the Fall Festival, Natalie approached Ashley in the hallway. They walked out to the front of the school and Natalie turned to her. "Ashley." She was quiet again. "I . . . want to apologize. For how I've acted since school started." Natalie paused. "You've been so nice. And . . . I don't know . . . I've been kind of mean."

Ashley was speechless. Which was becoming something of a habit. She wanted to say that Natalie had been more than "kind of" mean. But that didn't feel like the right response. Finally she found the words. "Natalie . . . you don't have to—"

"I have more. Please." Natalie took a slow

breath. "My dad . . . he's in the military." Her voice cracked, like she was holding back an ocean of tears. "He hasn't been home all year."

*All year?* "That's terrible." Ashley had heard of kids whose parents served the country. She decided to say what her parents always said. "Well, Natalie . . . thank you for serving."

Natalie hesitated. "I don't serve."

"Yes, you do." Ashley nodded. "Every day you miss your daddy, you're serving. Just like him."

"Okay." Natalie shrugged one shoulder. Probably because that did actually make sense.

Quiet came over Natalie again when they stopped walking. Finally she looked into Ashley's eyes. "I just miss him." Natalie took a long breath and continued. "We change cities a lot, too. So I don't do well meeting new people. I'm always afraid we'll move again." Her face looked sad. "And I'd have to start all over." She circled the toe of her shoe in the grass. "So thanks . . . for not giving up on me."

Ashley felt terrible for Natalie. All this time she had thought the girl was mean. But that wasn't true at all. Natalie was only sad. Sad and lonely. A long sigh came from Ashley. She thought for a minute. Then she stepped forward and hugged Natalie. That was all she could think to do.

Because sometimes there really were no words.

Then Ashley had an idea. Her friendship bracelet was on her own wrist—in case an unlikely class friend came along. And now finally, Ashley knew who to give it to. She slid the bracelet off. "Here." She gave it to Natalie. "I want you to have this."

Surprise came over Natalie. "For me? Really?" She slipped it on, and then she did something that shocked Ashley. Natalie took off the one *she* had made, which she was wearing, and she handed it to Ashley. "I thought I was the only one who hadn't given mine away." She grinned. "This one is for *you*."

Ashley put it on her wrist. "You're my unlikely friend, Natalie. And I have a feeling I'll be more glad about that every day."

"Me, too." Natalie bit her lip. She smiled. "Maybe one day we'll be *likely* friends."

"Yes." Ashley nodded. "That would be an improvement from what we've been."

Then something happened that Ashley hadn't expected. An action she had wondered if she would ever see in all of fifth grade. Not only did Natalie smile at Ashley's comment. She did something entirely new.

She laughed.

Saturday morning came and Ashley sat on her bedroom windowsill, watching the red and yellow leaves fall from the big tree out front. Something about the leaves reminded Ashley of herself. Changing colors. Trying to hang on. She watched another few leaves drift down. Did they struggle with letting go of the tree branch? Was change hard for them, too?

She pulled out her sketchbook and drew the tree. In her picture, some of the leaves were falling. The way she had been falling at first in fifth grade.

After she finished drawing, she looked out the window again. School was getting better all the time. But still on pretty days like this she missed Ann Arbor. More than anyone else in the family, apparently. She missed fourth grade and Miss Wilson and Samson the butterfly and Lydia. Lydia most of all.

She even missed Eric Powers.

Ashley turned from the window and put her shoes on. Maybe the issue wasn't this house or the city or the new school. Maybe it was her attitude.

Whatever it was, she wanted to work through it.

They were leaving in just a few minutes for the Fall Festival, and Ashley didn't want to be late. She hurried downstairs.

"Morning!" She jumped off the last step. Mom was sitting at the kitchen table. "Let the festival fun begin!"

"Good morning." Her mother sipped her coffee and smiled. "You're very happy today."

"Yes, I am." *See?* she told herself. *You can improve your attitude, Ashley Baxter!* It was her choice. "It's Festival Day, Mother!" Ashley stared at her mom, who was still smiling. All this time. "And what are *you* so happy about?"

"The Fall Festival, of course." Mom laughed. "I love fall. Can't get enough!"

The house smelled like cinnamon, but something was fishy here.

Just then the doorbell rang and Mom nodded at Ashley. "How about you get it?" Her eyes looked shiny. "Maybe it's a surprise!"

*A surprise?* Ashley's heart raced. *A surprise at the door?* It could be her gymnastics team, or Mr. Garrett and his wife, or the hair-cutter girl.

Ashley ran to the front door, and when she opened it, she nearly dropped flat on the floor. "Lydia!" Ashley couldn't get to her old friend fast enough. She hugged her before Lydia could say a word. "You're here! I can't believe you're here!"

"Me, too!" Lydia stepped back and looked up. "Your house is really pretty!" She hugged Ashley again. "I missed you so much."

Lydia's mom stood there, too. "Hi, Ashley! We thought we'd stop by!"

"This is the best stop by I've ever had!" Ashley squealed and held Lydia's hands and the two girls jumped and jumped around the porch.

After a while, they slowed down. It took a minute for them to catch their breath. Lydia looked at her for a while, right in Ashley's eyes. "You look . . . older."

"No." Ashley shook her head. "It's the hair. I had to cut it."

"Yeah." Lydia grinned. "Maybe that's it. I like it."

"Thanks." The gum story could come later. "But I guess we both look older." Ashley laughed a little. "Because we are."

Mom joined them. She put her arm around Ashley. "Lydia and her mom are driving to Kentucky later today for her uncle's wedding. They decided to come here first!"

Ashley's face lit up. "Lydia! You can go with us to the Fall Festival!" She jumped a few more times. "We can get caramel apples and take a hayride!"

Mom grinned. "For a few hours only. They're on a tight schedule."

"Then let's go!" Ashley shouted. She took Lydia's hand and, after a quick tour of their new house, they headed to the festival.

Downtown Bloomington's square was closed off to cars, which meant a million people could walk around everywhere without worrying about traffic. Ashley rode in Lydia's car, and she could feel her excitement building. "We love to come down here." She pointed at a brick building. "That's our favorite restaurant."

"Oooh." Lydia sat taller in her seat and looked at everything Ashley pointed out. "I think I love it here, too!"

They parked and started at one end of the square. Dad took Luke's hand, and Mom had Erin. Brooke and Kari walked together and Ashley stayed with Lydia and her mom. The sky was bluer than it had been all fall and the sound of fiddle music came from the main stage. The air smelled like sweet caramel and pumpkin spice.

Everything was decorated for fall. Pumpkins and hay bales marked the edges of the street and every now and then they passed booths with happy people selling muffins and cookies, jams and homemade crafts.

Lydia looked at Ashley. "You should sell your paintings here someday!"

The idea lit up Ashley's heart. "You're right!" She loved the sound of that. "I will definitely do that."

As they walked, Ashley told Lydia about her muddy day and how she had hidden behind her backpack.

Lydia giggled. "You're still the same Ashley Baxter." She touched the ends of Ashley's short hair. "What's the story here?"

So Ashley told her about Elliot and the giant gum tangle, and then about mean Chris and the unlikely friend she'd made in Landon Blake. Also how she'd gotten lost at the zoo with Landon and how they had made the best of it by becoming explorers. "And the happiest part—no handcuffs from the security guard."

Lydia had tears from laughing so hard. "I sure miss you, Ashley. There's no one like you back home."

"And"—Ashley gave her friend a sad smile—"there's no one like you here."

She told Lydia about Natalie and her dad serving in the military and about the Baxter children's adventures on the big rock behind their new house. "Also, sometimes . . . if you look real hard . . . the grass becomes green lava." Ashley gave a quick nod. "It's true."

The group stopped for pumpkin bread and then sat at a picnic table to eat it. Once they were situated, Ashley turned to Lydia. "How's our school? And how about that Eric Powers?" She rolled her eyes. "Still causing trouble?"

Lydia made a pensive face. "He changed schools." She shrugged. "Haven't seen him all year."

It took a minute for that sad news to sink in. Eric had changed schools? Did everyone and everything always have to change? Just like the leaves? Ashley sighed. "So . . . everything's different?"

Lydia shook her head. "Not everything." She grinned big. "I saw Samson the butterfly the other day! I came out for recess and he was right there . . . on the wall by my new classroom."

*Finally.* Ashley tried to smile. Something had stayed the same. "Of *course* he came back to you, Lydia. He came to me, too. You and me liked Samson the best." Ashley put her hand on Lydia's shoulder. "You tell Samson I said hello. And tell him not to leave." She hesitated. "Too many people do that."

The smile on Lydia's face melted a little and her eyes got soft. "I'll tell him, Ash. I will."

Once they started walking again Lydia took a deep breath. "I have a new class friend. Her name's Sarah. She's great." Lydia gave Ashley a nervous smile. "We're even planning the class fall party!"

Ashley swallowed that detail. "Wow." She tried to find the right sort of smile. "I'm sure she's not as good at planning parties as me."

"No." Lydia angled her head and kindness warmed her voice. "No, there's no one like you, Ashley." The girls skipped over to the craft tent, where they made wreaths of small squash and fall leaves. They laughed when Lydia spilled her glue and again when Ashley got glitter in her hair.

"I hope it comes out." Ashley raised her shoulders a few times. "I can't cut it any shorter."

Lydia and Ashley laughed so hard they could barely talk. And everything was exactly perfect. Two best friends together again.

Even if only for a short time.

# 20

## Finding Home

### ASHLEY

The group walked a little farther through the festival streets. Ashley's thoughts were crowding her mind today. The truth was, life had changed. She and Lydia had new friends and they were doing different things. And maybe that was just part of the sometimes hard journey of growing up.

Aching images kept filling Ashley's heart. Eric Powers and Ann Arbor and Lydia. Her special butterfly, Samson, and her old fourth-grade class. Even her old home. And at that exact moment, Ashley spotted Natalie.

"Hey!" Ashley called out. "Hey, Natalie!" Ashley waved. "Natalie, come meet Lydia!"

From a distance, Natalie's face lit up. Then Ashley noticed something. Her new friend was with her mom and . . . and a tall, strong man in an army uniform.

Ashley gasped. *Wait! Maybe this was—*

"Look who came home!" Natalie ran up with the man. They were holding hands and Natalie had never looked happier. "My daddy surprised me!" She hugged the man's waist for a long time. Like she might never let go. "Dad"—she smiled up at him—"this is my new best friend, Ashley!"

*New best friend?* Ashley couldn't believe it. What was this? She actually had a new best friend! And it was the most surprising friend of all.

"Hello." The man in the uniform had a deep voice. He shook Ashley's hand. "Nice to meet you, Ashley."

"Yes, sir." Ashley thought about her own daddy. What if he'd been gone all year? No wonder Natalie had been so quiet. Ashley looked at the man for a long moment. "Thank you for serving. I'm . . . glad you're home."

"Thank you." He nodded. "Me, too."

"And me!" Natalie was still hugging his waist. She was probably going to stay that way all day.

Natalie's daddy grinned at Ashley. "You must be something special if my little girl calls you her best friend." He kissed the top of Natalie's head. "I've been praying night and day that God would give Natalie a friend."

That thought took Ashley's breath. Natalie's father overseas fighting for freedom, but most concerned that his daughter would find a friend. And to think that she—Ashley Baxter—was the answer to his prayers.

The details filled Ashley's heart to overflowing.

Lydia came up then. "Ashley *is* special, sir." She linked arms with Ashley. "I can promise you that." Lydia smiled at Ashley. "She was my best friend last year."

At first Ashley was going to correct Lydia. Not her best friend *last* year. Her best friend forever. But she kept the thought to herself. She introduced Natalie to Lydia.

"Hi!" Lydia looked at Natalie's outfit. "I like your skirt!"

"Thanks." Natalie's smile looked good on her. "I'm gonna do a wreath with my parents." She waved. "Nice meeting you, Lydia." She turned to Ashley. "See you in class!"

"Bye." Ashley watched her go, and then she turned to Lydia. "Natalie's great." She was going to tell Lydia about the rocky start with Natalie.

But it didn't seem to matter anymore.

The girls were still carrying their wreaths as they hurried off toward the stage to meet up with the others. It was time for Brooke's school orchestra to perform!

While the music played, Ashley couldn't stop smiling at her oldest sister. Brooke looked like a professional. Like she'd been playing violin forever. Ashley glanced around. Her whole family was here, the way they had been for Kari's swim meet and Ashley's gymnastics competition.

Because that was how the Baxter family did things.

When it was over, they all gathered around Brooke. "Your part was beautiful!" Mom gave her a hug.

Dad kissed Brooke's forehead. "That's my girl." He grinned at her. "So talented."

Ashley smiled. Dad had a way of making them all feel special. She was glad her daddy didn't have to leave for another country.

After a few minutes, Brooke hugged their parents and ran off with her friends. Thirteen was very old, after all. Brooke was practically an adult.

The family and Lydia and her mom walked through the petting zoo, and after that they even got to pick out their own pumpkins. Ashley got a medium-size one. "Because my arms are still medium-size." She smiled at her daddy. "For now!"

Lydia's mom carried their pumpkin. "Well . . ." She sighed. "Time to go, I'm afraid."

"Okay." Lydia gave Ashley a sad look. "I wish we had more time."

Ashley set her pumpkin down, and gave Lydia a long hug. "I was thinking something this morning." She stepped back and put her hands on Lydia's shoulders. "When leaves have to let go of the tree, they wear their best colors and"—Ashley twirled—"they dance all the way to the ground."

"Mmm." Lydia giggled even as tears seemed to shine in her eyes. "I like that."

"Yes." Ashley caught her balance from the twirl. She smiled at Lydia. "I'm not going to be sad this time." She hugged Lydia again. "I'm going to dance through the day." She lifted her wreath. "With all my best colors."

Lydia looked at her, right to her heart. "Me, too." She paused. "Glad you're doing well without me. Really."

"And I'm happy you still have Samson. And Sarah."

The whole family was quiet, watching the friends say goodbye.

Just then Luke raised his hand. "Ashley, I can get some napkins for your tears."

Ashley laughed and patted her little brother's head. "No, Luke." She gave her family a happy look and then turned to Lydia again. "No crying. Not this time." One last hug and she waved goodbye.

"See you again one day, Lydia." Even though she tried not to cry, when she hugged Lydia a single tear made its way down her cheek. Ashley brushed it off with her sleeve.

"See you, Ashley!" Then her Michigan friend and her mother walked away and disappeared into the crowd.

"Okay!" Ashley blinked the tears from her eyes and grinned at her family. She held up her colorful wreath and did another few twirls. "What's next?"

Everyone had an answer. Caramel apples. The corn maze at the end of the street. The hay wagon.

Ashley let her thoughts settle as she walked with her family. Change would always happen and people would always leave. That was part of life. As they headed for the hayride, Mom came up beside her. "Are you okay?" She ran her hand over Ashley's glittery hair.

Ashley hesitated. What she had said earlier was the truth. She blinked back a few more unruly tears and took a deep breath. "Yes." She thought for a few seconds. "Lydia is doing great without me . . . and I am doing pretty great without her."

"Oh, honey." Mom stopped walking and faced Ashley. "That's not true." She looked sad.

"Yes, it is." Ashley smiled. She wiped the wet from her cheeks. "And that's okay."

"Wow." Mom leaned back a little, clearly surprised. "Look what God did! He helped you move on."

"Exactly." Ashley did another spin and a ballet-type move. "He's helping me dance through the changes in life." She held up her wreath. "Like autumn leaves."

An hour later, the family was finished with the festival. The afternoon had been so fun, but now more than anything Ashley only wanted to be one place. She took her mother's hand. "Mom?" She looked up.

"Yes, sweetie?" Their mother was so pretty. And she had been so patient with Ashley over these past few weeks.

Ashley squeezed her mom's hand and took a deep breath. "Let's go *home*."

The rest of the family kept walking and talking and laughing, headed for the van. But Mom stopped. Hope and light and tears filled her eyes. "Honey." She looked at Ashley. "Did you mean that? You want to go *home*?"

"Yes." Ashley's heart had never felt happier. "I do."

Mom pulled her close and they swayed around for a bit. Then her mother took a deep breath. "Okay!" She took Ashley's hand and they followed after the rest of the family. Mom's happiness became a little laugh. "Next stop . . . home!"

There was something about finally saying "home" that made Ashley realize a deep truth. This whole time, the house had been wonderful. Her room wasn't really too big, and her new school was actually pretty great. Her new teacher definitely cared about her. Bloomington was beautiful, and now a few kids actually wanted to be her friend.

Those things had never been the problem.

The problem had been her attitude.

Ashley had come here looking for trouble, and so she had found it. Lots of it, actually. But now that she was choosing to be happy, everything was better.

When they got home, Ashley found her sketchbook and some pencils, and tiptoed out to the back porch. This was something she wanted to do alone. She glanced down at the white wood floor and a soft laugh bubbled up from her heart. Painting this place had been the best first day.

*Dip. Wipe. Spread.*

Ashley walked to the porch railing and looked out. Beyond the Baxter house, the sun was setting. A glow shone on the grass and through the trees. Ashley inhaled and the beauty around her filled her soul. "God, you're quite the artist." She tilted her face to the sky. "I have a lot to learn from You."

She walked down the steps and around to the front of the house. When she was out into the field a ways, she turned and faced her home. "Guess what?" she whispered. "You're growing on me, my friend."

The air was crisp and golden sunlight splashed onto everything it touched. Peace came over Ashley and she felt herself relax. Ever since coming to Bloomington, she had wanted to go back home. But now, Ashley realized something.

Home had been here all along. Which meant she had done it. In the most unexpected ways and the strangest of situations she had actually done it.

Ashley had found home.

She dropped to the grass and opened her sketchbook. A fresh page for her fresh attitude. Then she took her best pencil and began to draw. The heavy wooden front door and the wraparound porch. The tall windows and the dark roof and shutters. She sketched every detail. And when she was done, she studied the image.

It was better than her drawing of the Michigan house.

Ashley let the fading sunlight wash over her face. It was official. She loved this place more than anywhere. She took a deep breath and watched the leaves dance to the grass around her. Yes, she and Bloomington were going to get along just fine.

The door opened and Kari stuck her head out. "Ashley! Dinner's ready! We're waiting for you!"

"Coming!" Ashley stood. She brushed the grass

off her legs and hurried toward the front door. Just before stepping inside, she stopped. She ran her hand over the wooden door. The door that would open up for birthday parties and family game nights and fall dinners. One that would lead to all the seasons ahead. Whatever they held, life on the other side of this door would be good.

Ashley had already decided.

She twirled once more and then walked inside. "I'm home!" she called out. Then she paused. The word felt sweet on her lips and warm in her heart. Because today, for the first time, it was true.

She was finally home.

# Finding Home

• Family Activity Guide •

As the Baxters say, your best friends are the people around the dinner table every night. Family time is such an important part of the day, a chance to share your life, talk through your feelings, and have fun with one another! Here are some fun facts and questions to discuss with your family and also a list of activities to do together.

## Did You Know?

- Bloomington, Indiana, has been ranked as the seventh smartest city in America.
- Most floor routines in gymnastics are done on a springy floor to help the athlete complete their tricks.
- The average high school swimmer swims one million strokes per season. Talk about a good workout!
- The best time to paint your home is when it's around sixty-five degrees outside.
- The San Diego Zoo in California is one of the largest zoos in the world. There are around 3,700 animals at this particular zoo. That's a lot of animal food!

## Questions for Around the Dinner Table

1.  Have you ever had a hard time meeting a new friend? What did you do?

2.  What is your favorite animal at the zoo?

3.  Ashley got embarrassed at the ice cream social when she accidently spilled ice cream on her teacher. Have you ever been embarrassed? How did you respond? What is the best thing to do when we get embarrassed?

4.  In the story, Mom and Dad talk about having an attitude of gratitude. What are you grateful for?

5.  If you could do swimming or gymnastics, which would you choose? Why?

6.  In one chapter, Ashley and Kari's mom helped someone who was in need. How can you help people who need it?

7. If your class took a field trip, where would you want to go?

8. God is always listening. Do you ever talk to Him? What do you say?

9. What is your favorite thing about your school?

10. Ashley likes to draw and Kari likes to journal. This is how they relax. What is your way to relax at the end of the day?

11. How would you describe your classmates and teacher?

## Activities With Your Family and Friends

1. Look for a special place in your home or neighborhood that is your "special rock"—a place to dream and pray and explore.

2. Get some friends together, either in your neighborhood or at recess, and play a game of kickball.

3. Draw a picture of doing something you love, like a sport, hobby, or after-school activity.

4. Make an unlikely friend at school and invite them to sit with you at lunch. Write about that experience.

5. Find a way to plan a birthday surprise for someone in your life. Make them a card, have an adult help you purchase a gift, or cook a treat for them. Be sure not to burn it!

6. Ask an adult to help you find directions on how to make a friendship bracelet. Complete the bracelet design. Then think of an unlikely friend to give it to.

Turn the page for a sneak peek at
*Never Grow Up.*

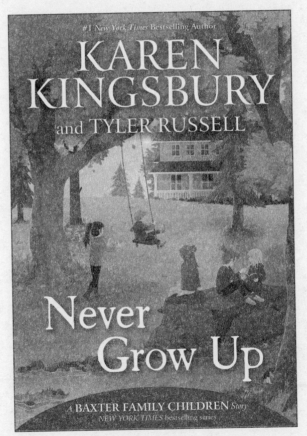

# Meteor Madness

## KARI

Kari Baxter's head was somewhere in the clouds.

Nothing very unusual about that. Kari was more of a dreamer than most kids in her sixth-grade class. Only this time being in the sky was the exact right place for Kari.

Her teacher, Ms. Nan, was talking to them about meteors. Not from a science fiction book. But actual balls of fire streaking through the real-life sky over their heads. Kari could hardly believe it.

Ms. Nan stood in front of the class. "Next month we'll have a meteor shower over Blooming-ton, Indiana." The teacher's eyes lit up. She was a big fan of meteors, apparently. She looked down the rows of students. "We'll do a countdown until then, and on that night each of you will spend an hour viewing the meteor shower from home."

Excitement welled up in Kari. An in-person meteor shower! Right here in Bloomington! She couldn't wait to tell her family. Her four siblings would also want to count down the days, Kari was sure.

She gazed out the window and imagined the night sky covered with streaking lights, and she couldn't stop smiling. Kari liked school. She was good at all her classes. But this wonderful news took learning to an entirely new level. Kari turned her eyes back to Ms. Nan and listened to every word.

"Boys and girls, I assure you this will be an unforgettable cosmic event." Ms. Nan sat on the edge of her desk. "Who has seen a meteor shower before and what do we know about them?"

Liza's hand shot up first. Liza was one of Kari's new friends, and her teammate on the school's swim team.

"You've seen a meteor shower, Liza?" Ms. Nan looked impressed. "Was that here in Indiana?"

"Well, not exactly." Liza enjoyed talking. "Last summer we went to Washington State for Fourth of July and my uncle set off a hundred fireworks." She made a grand gesture with both arms over her head. "All across the whole sky." Liza smiled and lowered her hands back to her sides. "And that, I believe, was very much like a meteor shower."

Ms. Nan blinked. Like she wasn't sure what to say. "I see." She nodded. "Very nice, Liza." She looked around. "Has anyone seen an actual meteor shower? With meteors?"

A kid named Jake raised his hand. He played drums in the school band. "Ms. Nan, aren't meteors falling stars?"

"Hmm." Their teacher tapped her knee. "Good thought, Jake. They are kind of like stars. Let me show you." She walked to the blackboard. "Okay." Ms. Nan drew a small circle. "Here we have Earth. That's us." She drew lots of smaller circles around Earth. "These represent other planets and stars. Even debris."

"Debris?" The question came from Mandy, who sat next to Kari. Mandy was another of Kari's friends, and also a fellow swimmer. Mandy never fell in the mud or got dirt on her dress at recess. She wrinkled her nose. "You mean . . . like trash?"

Ms. Nan turned to Mandy. "Well, kind of . . . There could be rocks, or comets and asteroids. This is typically what we call meteors." She drew some rocks with fire coming off of them. "A meteor shower is caused by streams of this natural cosmic debris entering Earth's atmosphere at extremely high speeds."

*High speeds?* A splash of fear hit Kari.

Up until that moment Kari had figured she would watch the meteor shower from the middle of their huge front yard. Or on the big rock by the stream behind their new house. The rock was flat and it was the best place for Kari and her older sister, Brooke, and her younger siblings—Ashley, Erin and Luke—to sit and talk.

But now she wasn't so sure. Maybe they'd be safer inside.

Kari raised her hand. "Ms. Nan . . . That sounds dangerous. What if meteors crash into Bloomington and we blow up?" Kari's heart beat harder. "Maybe we should take cover."

"Well . . ." Ms. Nan crossed her arms. "I suppose a meteor shower could be dangerous. But it isn't likely." She smiled. "I'd say we don't need to worry."

Kari tried to imagine how the event would look. "So as the rocks and garbage come into our . . . atmosphere . . . ?"

"Yes, atmosphere." Ms. Nan nodded. Patience was her strong suit. "*Atmosphere* will be one of our spelling words next week." She hesitated. "Anyway, yes, a meteor shower happens as rocks and *debris* enter our atmosphere."

"With flames around them?" Kari still wasn't convinced this was a good idea.

"Yes." Ms. Nan smiled. "Exactly."

"When is it?" Kari tapped her desk. "How many days?"

Ms. Nan laughed and walked over to her calendar. "Forty-one days. Just over a month."

Kari's shoulders sank a little. "So . . . Bloomington might be destroyed in forty-one days?"

"No." For a second, Ms. Nan laughed out loud . . . but then she seemed to get control of herself. "Kari. Bloomington will not be destroyed in this meteor shower. Scientists can predict that sort of thing."

Their teacher started talking about Mars and Jupiter, which gave Kari time to think. Ms. Nan wouldn't lie to them. Surely the meteor shower wouldn't destroy Bloomington. And that meant Kari could be excited again.

A real meteor shower right over their very own city!

"All right." Ms. Nan stood. "Let's do free reading now. Then after lunch we'll talk about our next assignment. It's called: *When I Grow Up*."

Kari's mouth went dry. *When she grew up?* Why would Ms. Nan want them to think about that? Sixth grade was hard enough without thinking about growing up. She raised her hand superfast.

"Yes, Kari?" Ms. Nan looked confused.

Kari swallowed. "Do we have to decide today? What we'll do when we grow up?"

"No." Something about Ms. Nan's voice made Kari relax. "You don't have to decide. I'll explain everything after lunch."

"Yes, Ms. Nan." Kari remembered to smile. She didn't want to panic, but she was struggling to get her head around this assignment. Sometimes she wasn't sure what she wanted to do next week, or what she wanted to have for lunch. The idea of trying to decide what she wanted to do when she grew up was scary.

She didn't know how else to put it.

When their teacher was back at her desk, Kari grabbed her journal from her backpack. Journaling was her favorite. She flipped through the pages until she found the next blank one and then, with a quick breath, she began to write:

> A meteor shower is coming to Bloomington! In just forty-one days! It sounds like the prettiest light show ever and I bet God has the best seat in the house that night. November 15. Yep. That's the day. Ms. Nan says not to worry that the flaming meteors will destroy our city. So that's good. Also, I have to think about growing up. It's our assignment this afternoon. But

the truth is . . . I have no idea what
I want to do. Dancing, maybe. Or soccer.
Here's my secret: I'm not even sure I like
being on the swim team, which I haven't
told Liza and Mandy. What if they don't
like me if I'd rather dance? I can't
think about it. Actually, maybe I'll study
meteors.

"All right." Ms. Nan stood. "Lunchtime." The
bell rang and the students lined up at the door.
Kari finished her journal entry.

Okay. I gotta go. Consider this the
official meteor shower countdown.
41 DAYS UNTIL THE METEOR SHOWER!

Get your copy of

*Never Give Up*

by Karen Kingsbury and Tyler Russell
to finish the rest of the story!

# About the Authors

Karen Kingsbury, #1 *New York Times*–bestselling novelist, is America's favorite inspirational storyteller, with more than twenty-five million copies of her award-winning books in print. Her last dozen titles have topped bestseller lists and many of her novels are under development as major motion pictures. Her Baxter Family books are being developed into a TV series. Karen is also an adjunct professor of writing at Liberty University. She and her husband, Donald, live in Tennessee near four of their adult children.

Tyler Russell has been telling stories his whole life. In elementary school, he won a national award for a children's book he wrote, and he has been writing ever since. In 2015, he graduated college with a BFA from Lipscomb University. Soon after, he sold his first screenplay, *Karen Kingsbury's Maggie's Christmas Miracle*, which premiered in December of 2017 on the Hallmark channel. Along with screenplays and novels, Tyler is a songwriter, singer, actor, and creative who lives in Nashville, Tennessee, where he enjoys serving his church, adventuring around the city, and spending time with his family.